"I love how Kathi Macias's b[...] [...] places on an adventure. But that adventure unfolds to reveal secrets and social injustices her characters have to navigate and expose. Through the eyes of Macias's fictional characters, I grow as a person. I love the rich settings and deeply moving situations in *A Christmas Gift.*"

—ANGELA BREIDENBACH,
Christian Authors Network president,
author, and national speaker

"What if a widow steps out of her comfort zone to serve in the volatile world of Mayan Mexico only to find that God's plans for her are far different than hers—and seemingly far more dangerous? This page-turning, cultural thriller is packed with compelling and sobering truths about the broken and sometimes evil world around us as well as the reality that God's plans are, ultimately, good. Kathi Macias delivers a heart-stopping and intriguing story of redemption that you won't soon forget."

—SUSAN G. MATHIS, author of
The Remarriage Adventure and *Countdown for Couples*

"*A Christmas Gift* shines with endearing characters, in particular, Julia. She will sing your song—of the loss one cannot bring back, the adventure that beckons, the adjustment that is inevitable. But through the heart-tugging journey, *A Christmas Gift* plays the melody of hope. The never-ending hope for a new life, a new land, and the sweetness of a new beginning."

—JANET PEREZ ECKLES,
author and international speaker

"The La Paz mission compound in southern Mexico could be exactly the change of scenery that high school teacher Julia Bennington needs. Certainly, they need her. But more awaits her in the remote jungles than wildlife and beauty.

A sinister grappling for her very life forces her to consider the reality of God's promises—and whether He will save her from imminent death.

"In *A Christmas Gift,* Kathi Macias takes her readers to the stunning rain forests of southern Mexico where American teacher Julia Bennington tries to do the right thing. The very thing that may end up taking her life.

"In the tradition of Kathi Macias's life-changing fiction, *A Christmas Gift* grips the heart as one woman's effort to do the right thing lands her in the clutches of unspeakable evil."

— DAVALYNN SPENCER,
author of *The Snowbound Bride*

"*A Christmas Gift* drew me in from the first page. I've been on over a dozen short-term missions trips in Mexico. I've not been to Chiapas, but I have been to areas much like the one that is the setting for the story. I love missionaries, and I love the Mexican people. All of these elements in the story were so true to the life that I've personally seen and experienced. I fell in love with the main characters, and the suspenseful storyline kept me turning pages until the end. I highly recommend this book."

— LENA NELSON DOOLEY,
award-winning author of the "McKenna's Daughters" Series, and screenwriter for the Higher Ground Films movie, *Abducted to Kill*

A CHRISTMAS G·I·F·T

Can a simple man and his faith be enough for her to stay?

Multiple Award-Winning Author

KATHI MACIAS

NEW HOPE
PUBLISHERS
Gospel-Centered. Missions-Driven.

BIRMINGHAM, ALABAMA

New Hope® Publishers
PO Box 12065
Birmingham, AL 35202-2065
NewHopeDigital.com
New Hope Publishers is a division of WMU®.

Library of Congress Cataloging-in-Publication Data

Macias, Kathi, 1948-
    A Christmas gift / Kathi Macias.
            pages cm
        ISBN 978-1-59669-416-3 (sc)
1. Christmas stories. 2. Christian fiction. I. Title.
PS3563.I42319C45 2014
813'.54—dc23
                        2014021838

ISBN-10: 1-59669-416-5
ISBN-13: 978-1-59669-416-3

N144122 • 1014 • 3M1

To my husband, Al,
and our family,
who always give me a reason to sing . . .
And to my Lord, who gives me the Song.

★ PROLOGUE ★

THE DARKNESS THAT ENVELOPED HER was more than simply the natural darkness that came from being blindfolded or even the realization that at any moment she could be killed and catapulted into an eternity she wasn't certain she was ready to face. Rather, it was an all-consuming darkness, so heavy and oppressive and terrifying that she struggled just to breathe. And, unlike the darkness of her worst nightmares, there was no hope of awakening to the sunlight streaming through her window or the songs of birds or even monkeys greeting the dawn in nearby trees. No hope of laying eyes on her beloved college-age children or parents. Those were sights and sounds she despaired of experiencing ever again.

Julia thought back to the minutes immediately preceding her kidnapping. She had felt so peaceful and serene, basking in the noonday sunlight that penetrated the thick trees and relishing the beauty of the colorful ti plants in the lush rain forest that surrounded the La Paz Compound. She had come to La Paz a few months earlier to teach children who otherwise had little chance of an education or of escaping the poverty that was so prevalent in the ancient Mayan culture of southern Mexico. If only she'd listened to her family's warnings and stayed in the States, where her life had been predictable and relatively safe, even if less than exciting. More importantly, if only she'd listened to the cautions of those within the compound, all of whom had been here much longer than she, and not ventured out alone beyond the compound's walls. Yet she'd done it several times before, though never on her own, and had never had a problem.

This time, however, the worst-case scenario had become a reality. She had been kidnapped—how many days ago she wasn't sure—and was being held for ransom. She had heard her captors say they were asking a million dollars for her safe return, much more than her middle-class parents or grown children could ever raise. Oh, how she regretted the anguish this must be causing them! How much worse when they received word of her death? For there was no doubt in Julia's mind that death was the only realistic end to her situation.

She'd already heard her captors talking about her, saying that if her family couldn't come up with the money, they might be able to sell her to the local *curanderos*, or shamans, for a human sacrifice. As terrifying as that thought was, she couldn't help but hear the question echoing in her heart: *Then what?* How shaky was her relationship with God? Would He forgive her many years of ignoring Him, of turning away from Him to pursue her own plans and purposes? And what if He didn't? Despite the ropes that bound her hands and feet to the hard chair where she'd been sitting now for longer than she could estimate, she trembled at the thought. Fresh tears flooded her eyes, wetting her already damp blindfold. Through a dry throat and cracked lips, she begged once more for mercy, but the only answer was laughter and a sneer about mercy not being part of the plan.

"*Por favor,*" she whispered. "Please! Just some water . . ."

Instead of receiving even a drop of water, a fist slammed into her left cheek, knocking her head to the right. Before she could cry out, welcome relief came in the form of unconsciousness.

★ CHAPTER 1 ★

JULIA LAWSON BENNINGTON had a wonderful childhood. An only child, she was raised by loving parents in a small but tidy two-bedroom home in the San Diego suburb of Imperial Beach, just a few miles from the border of Mexico and blocks from the seashore. But then, during her sophomore year of high school, her father had lost his job. Finding one that paid slightly more than he'd made at the previous one, he was thrilled to accept it and move his family an hour north to the thriving community of Temecula, where it was hotter in the summer, cooler in the winter, and an hour from the beach. That had been the hardest part for Julia—being too far away from the ocean to be able to walk there. The only thing worse was leaving her friends behind and trying to get reestablished in a new social environment—no easy task for any teenager.

But she'd managed, even adapting to the fact that she could no longer stroll the beach on a daily basis. Before long she made a few friends and began to enjoy the Old Town area of Temecula, as well as the lovely rolling hills—many of which were dotted with wineries—that surrounded the city of just over a hundred thousand. Upon graduating high school, she moved south again to attend San Diego State and to work toward earning her teaching degree. It was there she met Tom Bennington, one year ahead of her and also studying to become a teacher.

How her life had changed! It was the proverbial "love at first sight" for both of them. Although their families encouraged them to wait until after they'd graduated and gotten jobs, they opted for a small wedding during Tom's senior year and Julia's junior. Finances had been tough as they struggled to balance school and part-time jobs, but

Julia thought she'd never been happier than during the nearly three years they lived in that tiny studio apartment less than a mile from school.

She smiled now at the memory, as she sat on the comfy leather sectional in her spacious family room, her mind sorting through snapshots of happier times. Tom had called this room his "man cave," as he spent countless hours there watching college and pro football, munching on his favorite snack of caramel popcorn, and rooting for his favorite teams.

Julia's smile faded. Could she still consider this room a man cave, even though her man was no longer here? It had been two years since a heart attack claimed Tom's life, leaving Julia a grieving widow at the age of forty-six.

Two years. Two years of crying and telling myself to get over it, of avoiding well-meaning friends who keep wanting to set me up with someone else. Don't they understand? I don't want someone else. I want my husband back. Oh, Tom, why did you leave me? What am I to do with the rest of my life? How am I supposed to go on without you?

She picked up Tom's favorite sweater from her lap, burying her head in the soft knit and sobbing as she inhaled what was left of his scent. She knew she was being overly dramatic, that she certainly wasn't the first woman in history to lose a beloved husband. She knew too that she had much to be grateful for—two healthy parents nearby who loved and supported her and two grown children off at college beginning their own lives yet both attentive and loving to her. And she had her teacher's position, didn't she? Every year she welcomed a new crop of high school students, some rowdy, some studious, some downright obnoxious, but all needing to learn and mature. She was blessed to be part of that process, so how could she complain?

Her mind knew all that, but her heart refused to listen. She hated being a widow, hated living alone in a house full of memories that never seemed to let up, always tugging at her heart and her tear ducts. Would her life ever change? Would she ever experience laughter and joy again? Everyone assured her she would and she desperately wanted to believe them, But, right now, with her face buried in her late husband's sweater, she couldn't imagine how that could ever happen.

★ ★ ★

"JULIA? JULIA, where are you?"

The familiar voice eased her into consciousness, pulling her back from the fine line between daydreaming and actual sleep. She seemed to be spending more and more time there lately.

"In here, Mom," she called, clearing her throat. "Come on in."

Marie Lawson stepped into the doorway and stopped. "You've been crying again," she observed, resuming her approach until she sat down on the brown leather couch beside her only child. Her scarcely wrinkled face showed her concern as she laid a hand on Julia's. "You spend far too much time alone in here, thinking and crying." She paused. "You can't bring him back, you know."

"I know that, Mom." She hoped the trace of irritation she felt at such a pointless statement didn't come through in her words. She had no desire to hurt her mother, but there were times the woman overstated the obvious, and it got on her nerves.

Marie squeezed Julia's hand. "I don't doubt that you know it; I just wish you'd do something about it. You need to get out more."

Here we go again! "I get out plenty," Julia reminded her mother. "I have a job, remember? I go there five days a week."

Marie nodded. "True. But not in the summer. It's the first of May. What are you going to do during those weeks after school lets out?"

Julia's head began to pound. "I haven't had time to think about that yet, Mom. Right now I'm swamped with end-of-the-year school activities, grading finals . . ." Her voice trailed off. She knew it was a pitiful excuse for why she'd no doubt sit around all summer, weeping and feeling sorry for herself, but right now it was all she had to offer in hopes of staving off her mother's unwanted advice.

"It's not enough," Marie countered. "I know all that will keep you busy for a few more weeks, but then what?"

Julia wanted to reply that she would lock herself in her house and hide, but she wasn't about to open that can of worms with her mother. "The kids will be home," she said, grasping at that thought as she pushed a short lock of unruly red hair from her forehead. "They'll keep me busy."

Marie's smile was tentative. "Of course they will— to some degree. But you know Tyler will be working at his old job, delivering pizzas, like he does every summer. And Brittney is such a social butterfly. She'll spend most of her time catching up with her friends. So where does that leave you? What exactly are you going to do? Just sit around here, moping all day and waiting for them to drop in now and then so you can make them a sandwich?" She sighed and shook her head. "Honey, I know you miss Tom terribly. He was a wonderful man, and you two were so in love. But he's been gone more than two years now. You really do need to begin making a new life for yourself."

"Doing what?" Julia demanded, angry with herself for exploding at her mother, who only wanted the best for her, and yet unable to hold her feelings in any longer. "What would you have me do, Mom? Seriously. I'm forty-eight years old. I have a good job, a nice home, great kids—and until recently, a wonderful marriage. Isn't that enough? Why do I need more?"

Marie's gray eyes held a pained expression, but Julia knew it was for her daughter more than herself. "I'm sorry,

Mom," she said, her voice softer now. "I didn't mean to yell. It's just—"

"I know, dear." Marie patted Julia's hand. "I know you're lonely and hurting and brokenhearted, and what you really want is to have your life back the way it was before . . . before Tom died." She paused. "But that will never happen, sweetheart. And you can't spend the remainder of your life living in the past."

Hot tears bit Julia's eyes. It was one thing to know her mother was right, quite another to acknowledge it or to know what to do about it. "Don't you see, Mom? I have no desire to do anything else—anything but what I'm doing already. I work, I have you and Dad and the kids. At my age that's enough for me."

Marie shook her head. "I don't think so. You know, Julia, my friend Carolyn Barnes—you remember her, don't you?" She didn't wait for an answer. "She and her husband, Frank, are quite a bit older than you—in their early sixties—and they're venturing out into something new. In fact, you won't believe what they're doing." She smiled, as her words picked up speed, her enthusiasm showing as her eyes danced. "They've moved to Mexico—southern Mexico—where the Mayan culture is still very strong, and education and job opportunities are almost nonexistent. They've taken the position of directors at a small compound in Chiapas State, just outside the town of San Juan Chamula and not far from the larger city of San Cristobal de las Casas. They live and work in the compound, running a school for the children there, as well as a small church. They've made a five-year commitment. Can you imagine? At their age! But they believe it's what God has called them to do, so they rented out their house and just up and went. Isn't that amazing? They've been looking for at least one more teacher to come down and help them, but so far, no takers. Still, they seem so happy and content, so fulfilled. Every time I get a letter from them, they talk about how much they love their work there . . ."

Julia watched as much as listened to her mother's animated monologue, not so much absorbing the words as processing what the Barneses had decided to do. Teach in a faraway land, where children had little or no chance at education or a better life? It was something she'd dreamed of doing for years, even when she was in high school, long before she met and married Tom. She imagined that dream had long since been buried, but suddenly the flame seemed to flicker back to life.

"How did they find out about this place, Mom?" Julia asked, no doubt surprising her mother nearly as much as she surprised herself. "And what sort of teacher are they looking for?"

Marie's eyebrows shot up an extra notch, and she hesitated before answering. "I'm . . . not sure. Why do you ask?"

"Because I . . . I think I just might be interested in something like that. Seriously, Mom. You know it's something I wanted to do when I was younger, but I never imagined I'd have the opportunity. Besides, I met Tom and settled into my life with him. All other dreams went on the back burner then. But now . . ."

Marie's eyes were as wide as saucers now, and Julia knew her mother was regretting ever bringing up the subject. But it was too late. She'd already told her daughter about it and suddenly, inexplicably, Julia thought that just maybe there might be something more for her to do after all.

★ ★ ★

MARIE HAD REFUSED TO GIVE her daughter the Barneses' contact information, but Julia had tracked them down on one of her social networks. Apparently they had at least sporadic Internet service in this remote area of southern Mexico. If that was the case, how really *desolate* or *dangerous*—her parents' specific words as they tried to dissuade her—could the place actually be?

Julia caught herself humming as she searched the Internet for more info on the area. San Juan Chamula, the closest town to the compound, seemed to be somewhat of a tourist attraction. *It has to be a charming place, with its mixture of Mexican-Catholic influence and Mayan culture—even if they don't allow tourists to take pictures inside its main church or even of the Christmas procession on the way to the building. I can't wait to see it!*

She was especially intrigued with the descriptions of the curanderos, or shamans, men and women who practiced their ancient medicine throughout the area. Her parents' warning of rumors that some of them still practiced human sacrifice didn't faze her one bit. Only her mom and dad, with their strict evangelical beliefs, would even consider such a thing to be possible in this day and age. Besides, with all her research, she had yet to unearth any serious proof of such modern-day practices.

Gang violence throughout the country, however, was a real concern, though that seemed more prevalent in large cities than in such remote areas as San Juan Chamula. And with the school being inside the locked compound, she felt confident she would be safe.

Julia sighed. It was as if the possibilities had not only resurrected her youthful dream of teaching children in poverty-stricken areas of other countries, but it had breathed new life and hope into her as well. It seemed she would finally have a purpose again—the first time she'd sensed that since Tom died.

"How can you say that?" her mother had demanded when she'd tried to explain it to her. "What about the students you teach at the high school? Don't you think that gives you a purpose? And if you really want to teach in some poverty-stricken area, there are plenty of places right here in our own country. Why do you have to go so far away?"

But the more her parents argued, the more Julia was determined to follow through. Her initial contact with the Barneses had been encouraging, and she would be meeting with them when they came home in June for a brief vacation to take care of some business and to visit their grandchildren. Julia could hardly wait.

Meanwhile, she stayed busy tying up all the loose ends that went with wrapping up another school year. The students would no sooner walk across the stage to receive their diplomas, toss their caps into the air, and cheer their accomplishments than Brittney and Tyler would be arriving on Julia's doorstep. How she looked forward to seeing them again! But how would they react to her news? She had sworn her parents to secrecy so as not to spoil the surprise. She wanted to tell her children about her plans herself—in her own way and on her own time. Her parents would no doubt get to them soon enough and try to plant seeds of doubt and fear in their minds, but she hoped they would see her point of view and support her.

Regardless, if Frank and Carolyn Barnes agreed to take her on as a teacher in their compound, she was going—with or without the support of her parents. True, her children were still college-age and not really out on their own yet, but she would be gone less than a year. And they would have their grandparents to go to if they needed something. They would all just have to understand and trust that she knew what she was doing.

★ CHAPTER 2 ★

THE LATE AFTERNOON SUN was warm overhead, glinting off the red-gold curls that spilled down Brittney's back and shoulders. *Such a contrast to dark-haired Tyler— definitely his father's son.*

A stab of pain pierced Julia's heart at the reminder, but she blinked away the accompanying tears as she remained in her spot on the lounge chair under the tree. This was no time to start feeling sorry for herself. School was out for the summer, and her children were home. Though she knew they'd be busy with summer jobs and reconnecting with friends, she was determined to enjoy every moment she spent with them.

Today was no exception, as Tyler manned the grill, keeping a close eye on the chicken so it wouldn't burn. Brittney busied herself decorating the picnic table in vibrant summer colors, including fresh flowers, bringing a smile to Julia's lips. So typical of both of them—Tyler concerned with the practical, Brittney with the aesthetic. *But both are excited about getting everything ready for a cookout with their grandparents.*

"You just sit and relax, Mom," Brittney had told her as they started preparations a couple of hours earlier. "Tyler and I have got this covered."

From the looks of the bountiful spread now covering the table—including green salad, potato salad, beans, bread, and an assorted relish plate—she had been right. Of course, Julia's mom had never shown up empty-handed when it came to food, and today would be no exception. She would no doubt add to the pile of offerings that was already more than they could eat.

A CHRISTMAS GIFT

Julia frowned and glanced at her watch. *Mom and Dad should have been here by now. They're never late.*

As if on cue the glass door slid open and Marie Lawson stepped outside, carrying a hot dish and followed by her husband, John, carrying two more. Where would they put it all?

"We're here," Marie announced, ever the bearer of obvious tidings. "We would have been here sooner . . ." Her voice trailed off and she cast an accusing glance at John. "But someone had to see the end of the basketball game before we could leave."

John Lawson, tall and still fit for his age, grinned sheepishly. "It's the playoffs," he explained. "Some people just don't understand how important that is—especially in overtime!"

Tyler laughed and was the first to embrace his grandfather as soon as both grandparents had placed their food on the table. "I get it, Grandpa, believe me. I snuck inside to watch the end of the game too—in between turning the chicken." He moved to his grandmother then, as Brittney hurried into her grandpa's arms.

They're all so happy to see each other. I'm so blessed to have such a close and loving family. Julia rose from her perch and went to join the group hug.

"So glad everyone's here now," she said, chuckling. "Looks like we have enough food to feed everybody in the neighborhood. Maybe we should go door to door and invite them."

"Nonsense," Marie admonished. "You can't have too much food when you have hungry college students home for the summer." Her eyes sparkled as she looked from one grandchild to the other. She shook her head. "You two are surely growing up, aren't you? It seems like yesterday you were running around here, playing 'hide-and-seek' and sitting on our laps."

"Well, they're too big for that now," John said, easing down on the bench on one side of the groaning redwood table. "And from the looks of things, we'll all be a lot bigger before this day is through." He squinted his hazel eyes and glanced at his wife. "I told you we didn't need to bring more food."

Marie ignored him as she settled down on the bench on the opposite side of the table. "Trust me, everyone, none of this food will go to waste. And besides, leftovers are always the best part of any meal."

As the conversation continued while Tyler removed the chicken pieces from the grill and placed them on a serving platter, Julia did her best to join in the festivities. She really was happiest when her family was around her, but it was also a constant reminder that her husband wasn't. Would she ever get past that? She doubted it, but maybe the trip to Mexico would help.

Tyler was busy regaling his grandparents with his football accomplishments as bowls and platters of food made the rounds. His voice became a buzz in Julia's ears as she wondered how she would tell them of her plans. She'd already met with Frank and Carolyn Barnes when they were in the States a week earlier, and they were thrilled that she wanted to come. The position was hers if she wanted it—she just needed to let them know as soon as possible so they could plan accordingly.

Julia grabbed a couple of carrots sticks as the relish plate passed by. She hadn't even told her parents how far along she was with her plans. Though she had yet to formally accept the Barneses' offer, she was definitely leaning in that direction.

"Mom, the potato salad. Mom?"

Brittney's voice cut into her thoughts, and she blinked as she turned her head toward her daughter. "I'm sorry, honey. What did you say?"

Brittney raised her perfectly shaped brows, reddish-gold like her long curly hair, and said, "The potato salad. Could you pass it, please?"

"Oh, of course." Julia reminded herself to stop day-dreaming and focus on her time with her loved ones. She quickly picked up the bowl and handed it to her daughter. As the meal and chitchat continued, Julia determined not to drift off again.

"Well, I'm just glad you two are home to keep your mom company for a while," Marie observed, smiling at her two grandchildren who sat across from her, next to their grandfather.

Julia, seated beside her mother, turned toward her. "I thought you said they'd be too busy with their own lives to keep me company this summer. Did I miss something?"

Marie frowned, her cheeks flushing slightly. "I just meant that . . . they're here, that's all. At least you're not alone in this house all summer."

Julia nodded. "Exactly what I tried to tell you when we discussed this a couple weeks ago. I'm glad you're finally seeing it my way."

"It's just . . .," Marie hesitated before plunging ahead, "it's just that I do want to see you get involved in something besides work. It's not enough. I told you that, and I still feel that way. But I certainly don't want you traipsing off to teach school in some dangerous, far-off place." She shook her head. "No, that's not an option. There are plenty of things to keep you busy right here in your own neighborhood. Why, you could volunteer at the senior center or—"

Before Marie could come up with another option to safely occupy her daughter's spare time, Brittney interrupted, fixing her green eyes on her mother's face. "Wait a minute. What's this about you teaching school in another country? This is the first I've heard about it. What's up, Mom?"

This time it was Julia's turn to blush—not so much with embarrassment as with anger. Hadn't she sworn her parents to secrecy until she could tell her children what she was considering? But it was out now; she might as well deal with it head-on.

"Actually," she said, taking a deep breath and squaring her shoulders just a bit, "I'm seriously considering going to Mexico to teach at a remote compound near San Juan Chamula. It's in Chiapas State, the southern part of the country. The people are very poor and have little opportunity for a good education. I—"

Marie laid her hand on Julia's arm. "So you're still thinking about going? I thought surely you'd given up on that idea by now."

"Not at all, Mom." After a quick glance at her mother she turned her attention back to the three people who sat across from her, all seemingly transfixed by her words. "In fact, I met with the Barneses when they were here last week, and they've extended a formal invitation for me to join them for one school year. I'd have to work things out with the school district here, but they're usually open to things like this, and they have plenty of time to find someone to take my classes for the next year."

"Mom, this doesn't exactly sound safe." Tyler's dark brows were nearly drawn together into one as he spoke. "I don't like the sound of this at all. Why would you want to go teach somewhere in a compound? I can see wanting to teach abroad somewhere, but Chiapas? Really? Isn't that where the Mayan influence is so strong?"

"It is," Brittney chimed in. "I've studied that area and culture, and outsiders are definitely not welcome there. I don't think you should go, Mom. I really don't."

"Neither do we," John Lawson chimed in. "Your grandmother and I have tried to dissuade your mother, but apparently we haven't done a very good job." He fixed a determined stare on his daughter. "Tell me you haven't accepted, Julia, that it's not too late. Please tell me you haven't and that you can drop this foolishness right here and now, once and for all. If it's a trip you need, I'll buy you an airline ticket—or a cruise to some exotic island. But almost a year in a place like that? Absolutely not. I won't allow it."

Julia's face grew hotter by the moment. How old did her father think she was? He was talking to her as if she were ten years old. And she didn't appreciate it one bit.

"I'm afraid it's not for you to allow or disallow, Dad," she said, her voice firm, though she had to clasp her hands together in her lap to keep them from shaking. "I'm a grown woman, and I can make my own decisions. And for your information . . ." She paused and looked around the table, catching each person's eyes in the process. "I have just decided to accept. I'll contact Frank and Carolyn Barnes today and let them know. I'll be leaving as soon as Tyler and Brittney go back to school."

A stunned silence fell on the group, and Julia found herself wondering if she'd made a terrible mistake. But she wasn't about to admit that to her parents or her children. She'd made an announcement, and she would stick to it.

She was going to Mexico to teach, period. Now she had to get the details squared away so she could begin her new adventure as soon as possible after Tyler and Brittney returned to college.

★ ★ ★

THE EMERGENCY FAMILY GATHERING had been initiated by John Lawson and orchestrated in such a way that Julia wouldn't realize what was going on behind her back. John had even stayed home from his job as a construction foreman to enable them to meet during the day. Hurried cell phone texts, sent almost immediately after John and Marie left Julia's home after the barbecue, had nailed everything down for the following day. Brittney had canceled her planned get-together with a couple of friends in order to ride with Tyler to their grandparents' home.

The early afternoon heat was already intense enough to require the old Toyota Corolla's AC to work at full force as they navigated the three-mile drive through the well-kept, older neighborhood. Brittney stared out the window as Tyler drove. Since they'd already had the "I can't believe Mom is even thinking about this" conversation the previous evening, she didn't feel the necessity to talk now. Apparently Tyler didn't either, as he had cranked up his favorite rock station, which precluded conversation of any kind. It certainly wasn't Brittney's choice of music, since she preferred classical or country, but she figured she could ignore it for the few minutes it took to arrive at their destination.

As they pulled into their grandparents' driveway and Tyler shut off the engine, they sat for a moment until Brittney turned toward her brother and broke the silence. "Are you ready for this?"

His face was grim as he nodded. "Absolutely. There is no way we can let Mom do something so crazy. Doesn't she remember that we just lost our dad a couple of years ago? Is she trying to make orphans out of us or what?"

Brittney raised her eyebrows, surprised at the twinge of guilt she felt as Tyler's words impacted her. It was the first time it had occurred to her that maybe this situation wasn't all about her or Tyler after all—or even about her grandparents. Maybe it was something their mother really needed to do for herself.

The thought unnerved her, and she grabbed the door handle. "Let's go. Grandma and Grandpa are waiting." But even as they stepped out into the ninety-degree heat, she frowned at the new direction her thoughts were taking her.

★ ★ ★

MARIE HAD INSISTED on preparing lemonade and serving the butter cookies she'd made that morning—anything to keep her busy until her grandchildren arrived and they could get this meeting underway. Since the first time Julia had mentioned the idea of checking into this teaching possibility, Marie had scolded herself for opening her big mouth. *It's all my fault,* she'd told herself over and over again. *If I just hadn't said anything about what the Barneses were doing down in Mexico . . .*

Then she'd increase her efforts at praying and begging God to stop Julia in her tracks. *She's not even serving You, Lord,* she'd remind Him. *It's not like she'd be going as a missionary which would be dangerous enough—though I think I could probably accept that. But . . .*

Now that Julia had formally announced her intentions, Marie felt twice as bad. She'd even told her husband she was going to try to get hold of the Barneses and tell them to turn down Julia's application. That's where John had drawn the line.

"No," he'd declared as they drove home from Julia's the previous evening. He'd even shaken his head in emphasis. "That wouldn't be right. She's an adult, after all, and God knows the purposes He has for her." He'd stopped to glance at Marie briefly before returning his eyes to the road. "We've always prayed that God would do whatever was necessary to bring Julia to a total commitment of her faith. If this is part of it—which could very well be possible—who are we to stand in the way?"

Before she could protest, he'd continued. "Now, don't get me wrong. That doesn't mean I want her to go. In fact, I plan to do everything I can to dissuade her. And I'll certainly be praying to that effect. I've even been thinking that we should invite Tyler and Brittney over to talk about this, as soon as possible. It's obvious they aren't any crazier about this idea than we are."

And so the meeting had been set. Marie fussed with the place settings at the table as they waited for their grandchildren's arrival. She doubted anyone was all that interested in lemonade or cookies, but then again, she'd never known Tyler to turn down a snack under any circumstances.

Within moments of hearing the doorbell, Marie had everyone seated around the table, sipping cold drinks and munching cookies—except for her. She was the only one who couldn't bring herself to join in. She wanted to get on with the reason for their meeting and find a solution to their problem.

"So," John said at last, setting down his half-empty glass. "We've reviewed the weather and all the other non-issues. Shall we tackle the elephant in the room?"

Tyler's previously animated expression changed, his dark eyes losing their sparkle. "Yeah," he said. "I don't like this one bit. Where in the world did Mom get such a crazy idea?"

Marie felt her cheeks grow hot, but before she could open her mouth to take responsibility, John intervened.

"The Barneses are friends of ours from church. Your grandmother mentioned what they were doing, never imagining your mother would be interested. We've been concerned about her continued depression since your dad died, but as far as her job went, we thought she was perfectly content teaching at the high school. Quite obviously we were wrong."

Marie glanced at her husband, and when their eyes met she knew he understood her silent but grateful message. She was so blessed to have such a loving partner, and she could certainly understand how lonely her daughter was since her own husband had died. Still, did that mean she had to travel so far away and put herself in mortal danger to try to ease the pain?

"Before we get started, can I say one thing?" Brittney asked.

Her grandfather's bushy salt-and-pepper eyebrows lifted, and then he nodded. "Of course you can, sweetheart. What is it?"

"I've been thinking about this nearly nonstop since yesterday, and I absolutely do *not* want Mom going there, period. But . . ." She hesitated, and Marie noticed her cheeks flush before she continued. "But it just occurred to me that maybe we're making this too much about us—the four of us, I mean—and not enough about Mom. This really is her decision, and . . ." She paused again, taking a deep breath before going on. "And besides, you both are always telling us how we have to trust God with our lives. I know Mom and Tyler and I aren't exactly into the church thing the way you two are, but still . . ." She frowned, her green eyes taking on a deep intensity as she looked from one grandparent to another. "Isn't this one of those cases where we're just going to have trust God with whatever Mom decides? Because deep down, even though I don't want Mom to go, it feels wrong to try to stop her just because we're afraid of what might happen to her."

Hot tears pricked Marie's eyes, and she did her best to blink them away. How long had she and John prayed, not only for Julia but for their grandchildren, wanting nothing more than to see them serving God in whatever way the Lord had purposed? Her heart raced at the implications, as she turned toward her husband. John's face had paled, as their granddaughter's words hung in the air between them.

Tyler was the one to interrupt the silence, anger shining in his eyes as he spoke. "No way, Britt. No way. I don't even want to hear this. What kind of God would send Mom to some heathen place to teach people who don't even want her there?" He shook his head. "I'm not buying it. No way."

Marie's heart ached as she looked from one grandchild to the other. Her spirit knew Brittney was right, but her mother's heart cried out to agree with Tyler.

★ CHAPTER 3 ★

CAROLYN BARNES'S SHORT GRAY CURLS frizzed as they always did in the humid climate of the rain forests of southern Mexico. The day had started with scarcely a breath of breeze, making the heat even more oppressive. But Carolyn didn't mind. As she sat with her husband on the tiny patio in the shade of the gum tree outside their one-room cottage during their brief lunch break, she thought as she had so many times before that she'd never been so blessed before.

She leaned her head back against the rough back of her wooden lawn chair and closed her eyes. One of the few Mexican customs that seemed to be observed even in this remote area of Mayan territory was the afternoon *siesta*. Before coming to the La Paz Compound a few months earlier, Carolyn had always insisted she couldn't take naps. Now she knew better. With the long hours they kept, overseeing not only the educational aspects of La Paz but the financial and business end of it too, afternoon siestas had become as much of a necessity as they were a luxury. Thankfully, Padre Ramon was with the children during part of the school day, including siesta time, so Carolyn and Frank could have a little time to themselves.

The familiar sounds of chirping and trilling birds, and even an occasional monkey call from the nearby forest, faded into the distance as the warm temperature lulled her to sleep. Her husband had nodded off beside her soon after finishing his lunch of vegetables and fruit. In a place somewhere between waking and dreaming, she called up a portrait of Julia Lawson as a teenager, for that's when she had first met her. Their recent meeting with Julia nudged her semiconsciousness with the fact that the woman no longer looked

A CHRISTMAS GIFT

the same, as she was decades beyond her teens now, but dreams seldom adhered to such logic. Even at forty-eight Julia was a beautiful woman, though with a veil of sadness marring her smile. Now, in Carolyn's vision, Julia was young again and appeared to be sitting on a church pew, alone, deep in prayer. Yet Carolyn recognized that the lovely young girl with reddish-blonde locks trailing down her back was agitated. Julia raised her head, and Carolyn saw tears on her makeup-free cheeks. In that moment Carolyn knew Julia was wrestling with God about her future. Carolyn tried to open her mouth to encourage the younger woman to listen to God and follow Him wherever He led her, but no words came out.

And then she heard the cry from somewhere outside her dream, jerking her back to the present. She opened her eyes, a chill passing over her at the recognition of the sound, even though it had already stopped. Carolyn had yet to see one of the rare jaguars the locals swore prowled the surrounding jungles, but she was certain she had heard them on occasion. This seemed to be one of those occasions, though she couldn't be certain.

She glanced sideways toward her husband. He too was stirring, opening his eyes and sitting up straighter in his chair.

"Did you say something, sweetheart?" he asked, turning to offer her a smile.

"No, nothing." She smiled back, amused that he would mistake the cry of a wild animal for his wife's familiar voice. "But I suppose it's time to get back to the office, isn't it?"

Frank glanced at his watch and nodded. "It is. As usual we have more things to accomplish than we have time. I'm looking forward to the cavalry arriving soon."

Julia. The memory of her dream flashed through Carolyn's mind as she nodded. Yes, having a full-time teacher on the premises was going to take a lot of pressure off them, despite the fact that she wouldn't be arriving until the first week of September—still more than a month from now— after her two grown children had returned to college. Padre

Ramon, who pastored the small La Paz church within the compound, one of the few evangelical churches in the area, was a big help to them on many fronts, but he didn't really have the time or the expertise to teach in the school, though apparently he had filled in on occasion. Carolyn thought the four of them would make a good team as they moved the mission of La Paz forward to fulfill God's purposes in the region.

La Paz. She smiled. *The Peace. A perfect name for such a little refuge in the middle of such illiteracy and pagan practices. Thank You, Lord, for allowing us to be a part of it.*

And with that she rose from her seat to gather the few supplies she would need for the afternoon school session.

★ ★ ★

JULIA WAS MORE CONCERNED with putting up with all the naysayers over the next few weeks than she was with how much she had to accomplish to be ready to leave by the first week of September. She'd made the arrangements regarding her job, with the blessings of the school administration, which looked favorably on their faculty spending occasional time teaching in other countries, and the rest of the preparation seemed minimal to Julia. But the constant barrage of warnings and even pleadings from her children and parents was getting tiresome.

Now, the first weekend of August, she hoped her family would focus on enjoying their time together at the beach, rather than trying to dissuade her from what she'd already decided and committed to do. Since leaving the San Diego area and moving to Temecula with her parents decades earlier, she'd relished any opportunity to escape to the coast, whether for a few hours or a few days. When her dad suggested they all rent a cottage right on the oceanfront in nearby San Juan Capistrano, she'd heartily agreed. Capistrano was one of her favorite places, full of rich history, delightful secondhand and antique shops, and absolutely delicious cuisine.

They had arrived at the cottage on Friday evening; by Saturday morning Julia was already looking forward to eating at her favorite Mexican restaurant, famous for its delectable offerings and also for the fact that former presidents and other celebrities had made a practice of eating there.

This morning she strolled the beach alone, carrying her flip-flops in one hand as she waded through the gently lapping waves, the water cool but invigorating. Even the weather had cooperated, its usual morning fog already burning off to allow the sun's warm rays to shine down on her.

I must admit, I'll miss this down in Mexico for a year. But rain forests have their own beauty too—something I've never seen before. Besides, it's time for me to have a new adventure. Tom would want me do it. . . . Wouldn't you, Tom?

She frowned at her slight hesitation, but pushed on. *Of course you would. You always told me I should enjoy life more—try new things, go new places, meet new people. Well, I'm sure going to be doing that now.*

Her heart constricted at the thought of how much nicer and more exciting it would be if she and Tom were going on this adventure together. But they weren't, and that was that. They would never again go on any sort of adventure together, and she simply had to get used to it. If there was to be any adventure in her life, any joy at all, she was going to have to step out on her own and make it happen.

And so she would. Her family could support her or not, but her mind was made up. In just over a month she would be flying off to teach students English as a second language—though her Spanish was slightly less than fluent—and math and science and any other classes they cared to study. The language issue would be one of many challenges she would encounter, of that she was certain. But it was one the Barneses had assured her she could quickly overcome.

Ignoring a gnawing sense of inadequacy, she turned and began the trek back to the cottage. The rest of the clan should be waking up about now, and her growling stomach told her she was more than ready for some breakfast.

★ ★ ★

PADRE RAMON WAS BUSY preparing for the Sunday service. Though his little flock scarcely numbered more than twenty-five or thirty, that was an improvement over the ten or fifteen they'd had just six months or so earlier. The mixture of Catholicism and Mayan superstition that prevailed in the area made it difficult for evangelicals—*los evangelicos,* as the locals called them—to make much headway when preaching the gospel. And it was more than simple apathy or mistrust of strangers. The indigenous people trusted the curanderos, or shamans, to be their spiritual leaders. Evangelicos were considered enemies to the old Mayan ways and were therefore unwelcome.

Still, Ramon felt blessed to pastor the little La Paz congregation, and his church had never been attacked or burned—unlike others that had tried to get established in the area. Because his family lived inside the compound, in a couple of rooms attached to the chapel, he had not been personally threatened.

The memory of Rosa, his wife of fifteen years, brought sudden tears to his eyes, but he blinked them away and continued to spruce up the little sanctuary, dusting and polishing the dozen wooden pews. His beloved Rosa, the mother of his three young children, had been attacked when she ventured too far into the jungle to gather fruit for breakfast. One of the curanderas, a woman who despised evangelicos, led a group of three men into the jungle where she had spotted Rosa. By the time the posse of four returned, Rosa lay dead on the jungle floor. Ramon hadn't been able to find her for two days. By then her body had been defiled by animals.

Five years had passed since that terrible time, and the tears returned as he walked to the front of the sanctuary to ready the Communion elements. This time he didn't blink them away but allowed them to drip freely onto his cheeks. It had taken his wife's death to convince Ramon to move with his children into the compound, where they already attended school. With the help of the couple who then served as directors at La Paz, Ramon had built the little chapel in Rosa's honor.

"*Aye, mi amor,*" he cried aloud, "will I ever stop missing you?"

He swiped at the tears with the sleeve of his worn, white shirt. "*Ayudame, El Señor,*" he whispered, bowing his head. "Help me, God. Help me to trust that Rosa is safe in Your care, and that for now You have purposed me to continue here, serving those who so desperately need to know You. *Gracias!*"

★ CHAPTER 4 ★

THE WEEKEND AT THE BEACH had passed far too quickly, though Julia relished every moment, especially those spent with her children. How she ached at the memories their time together stirred up, as she thought back on the many instances over the years when she and Tom had taken their children on outings to the beach. From the time Tyler and Brittney were toddlers they had loved the water, frolicking in the waves and digging in the sand until their parents had to pick them up and carry them home at the end of the day. Not much had changed. As the five of them enjoyed the time together in San Juan Capistrano, Tyler and Brittney had spent more time in the water than anywhere else. Julia and her mother had opted for shopping at the many antique stores lining the streets of the charming seaside town, and John Lawson had devoted himself to naps and reading on the patio.

At least Mom behaved and didn't spend too much time harassing me about my trip. Julia sighed as she unpacked her suitcase and added her sandy clothes to the huge mound already piled up beside the washer and dryer.

She smiled. Loads of laundry or not, it was wonderful having her children home again, even if only for a few weeks. The thought occurred to her that she hadn't thought to ask the Barneses about laundry facilities at the compound. Somehow she doubted they had the amenities that most Americans expected, both at home and abroad.

One more challenge to face when I leave next month. She took a deep breath to quell a sudden flutter of anxiety. *I'll be fine. I really will. It's just a matter of adjusting, that's all. It'll be good for me.*

She dumped a cup of soap into the already filling washer and began to check pockets as she added the clothes. How many times had she done this for her family over the years? She couldn't begin to estimate, but she was grateful for each instance, as it represented the love she had for her husband and children.

Tom. I still miss washing your clothes, and setting your place at the dinner table, and . . .

She shook her head. No. This was not the time to get caught up in melancholy again. Right now she needed to concentrate on enjoying her children while they were still home. In addition, she had a few vaccinations to get before she could leave, but at least her passport was current.

She picked up her now empty suitcase to replace it in the hall closet, reminding herself that in a couple of weeks she'd have to retrieve it, as well as a couple more suitcases from the attic, and start packing for her trip.

The Barneses assured me I don't need to bring anything fancy—just comfortable, functional clothes. But it's hot and humid in the summer months, cool in the winter. I'll need to keep that in mind.

"Mom, what's for dinner?"

Tyler's voice, calling down to her from upstairs, was so much like his father's. The reminder of her dead husband jolted her, but she smiled at her son's never-ending hunger. They'd had a late lunch on the way home from San Juan Capistrano. She glanced at her watch and smiled again.

That was almost three hours ago. Must seem like forever to him.

"Let me see what I can find," she called back to him. "Just need to finish getting this laundry going."

She sighed. Once a mom, always a mom. But soon her "little ones" would be back at school and wouldn't need her to throw together last-minute meals or snacks. So why not fly off to another country and culture where she could be useful to someone else's children for a while?

Nodding in agreement with her thoughts, she closed the lid to the washing machine and headed for the kitchen.

★ ★ ★

THE MONTH FLEW BY, with August heat in full swing. Cookouts were relegated to evening hours, and Julia spent most of her days sitting inside in the air-conditioning. Tyler and Brittney slept in nearly every morning, sometimes not stirring until nearly noon. But Julia didn't bother them about it. After all, their class schedule would have them up early soon enough.

To their credit, the two young people spent at least some of their time with their mother and grandparents, though Tyler was busy delivering pizzas for extra money whenever he could, and both of them hung out with their high school friends regularly. Julia was relieved that their objections to her plans—as well as her parents' vocal concerns—had faded. Still, she knew none of them were actually supportive, and they certainly weren't enthusiastic. But at least it seemed they'd made peace with it.

She had begun to pack even before Tyler and Brittney returned to college. Partially filled suitcases lay open on the couch in the seldom-used living room because the family preferred to gather in the "man-cave" to visit and watch television. Marie had blanched at the sight of the luggage the first time she'd wandered into that room, but she had pressed her lips together in a tight line and said nothing. Julia appreciated her mother's restraint.

But now it was time to say good-bye to her children as they loaded their belongings into Tyler's Toyota for the one-hour drive back to campus. It had never seemed so difficult before, because Julia knew then they would be back for Thanksgiving, if not sooner. But this year if they came home for the holidays, it would be to stay with their grandparents. Julia's heart wrenched with serious self-doubt at the sharp reality that she would not see her children for quite some time. Had she made a terrible mistake?

Fighting tears, she nearly melted into Tyler's embrace as he pulled her close for a last good-bye. Julia knew they planned to stop at their grandparents' house on the way out of town, but this was it for her.

"I'll miss you," she whispered, choking back a sob.

"I'll miss you too, Mom." Tyler's hug grew stronger. She wondered if he wrestled with begging her to change her mind. When he didn't, she couldn't be sure if she was relieved or disappointed.

And then there was Brittney. The lovely young woman's eyes glistened with tears as they gazed at one another, then hugged and kissed. "We've gotta go, Mom," Brittney said before pulling away and hurrying to the passenger side of the car.

Julia let her tears trickle freely down her cheeks as she watched the old blue Corolla disappear around the corner.

★ ★ ★

THE GOOD-BYES WITH HER PARENTS when they dropped her at the Los Angeles International Airport in the predawn hours had been nearly as painful as with her children. But now she was on her way, her two bulging suitcases checked in and her overnight stowed beneath the seat in front of her. She would fly into Angel Albino Corzo International Airport in Tuxtla Gutierrez and then transfer to a smaller flight to Copalar Airport in Comitan, where the Barneses would pick her up and drive her the final fifty miles to the compound. Her stomach churned as the engines droned, taking her farther and farther from the familiar, into the unknown experiences that lay ahead of her. She knew her mother had ached to beg her to reconsider, but she'd managed to hold it inside as her father held her close and prayed for her protection. And then they were gone . . . and she was alone.

It would be several hours before she connected with the Barneses. Assuming both flights were on time—and she had been informed that it might very well not be the case—she would be on her own until nearly dark that evening. She had a new novel and several snacks packed into her carry-on, plus her cell phone and charger, but she also knew that cell phone reception could be spotty in other countries. The Barneses had cautioned her that there were only two places in the compound where her phone would occasionally work and that Internet reception came and went, regardless of where you positioned your laptop. Still, she held out hope of being able to send and receive emails with her children and parents, as well as friends and co-workers. As much as she had insisted on her need for this new adventure, there was a big part of her that also needed to maintain at least some ties with home.

She leaned her aisle chair back and closed her eyes. Maybe if she caught a few winks the time would pass quicker. Before she could even hope to drift off, small feet began kicking the back of her seat.

"Stop that," a woman's voice hissed. "You'll bother the lady in front of you."

The kicking stopped for a few more moments before resuming. This time the woman issued no reprimand. Julia sighed and gave up on sleeping, choosing instead to reach under the seat in front of her to retrieve her carry-on. She pulled out her novel and stretched up to push on her reading light.

"Good book?"

The voice came from the elderly woman to her right, sandwiched in between Julia and the old man in the window seat. Julia had noticed them when she boarded the plane and nodded a greeting when she took her seat. She imagined they were married.

She smiled and turned to the woman. "I really don't know," she answered. "I haven't started it yet."

"Ah." The woman's faded blue eyes sparkled. "But that's the best part, isn't it?"

Julia frowned. "I'm . . . afraid I don't know what you mean."

"The beginning of a book." She smiled, causing her already sparkling eyes to dance. "It's like starting a brand-new adventure into the unknown. You have no idea where it will take you, but isn't it exciting to find out?"

Julia had never thought of a new book in quite that way, but it seemed more than appropriate at the moment. She nodded. "I suppose you're right."

"I'm Mona," the woman said. She tilted her head slightly toward the man beside her, who stared out the window. "This is my husband, Richard. We're flying to Mexico to visit friends in Tuxtla Gutierrez for a week. What about you?"

Julia's heart raced, though she couldn't imagine why. The woman had simply asked her a question. Why should that cause anxiety? "I'm actually going on from Tuxtla Gutierrez to Comitan, where some friends will be picking me up. They direct the La Paz Compound near San Juan Chamula. I'm joining them for nearly a year to help with teaching."

The woman's face lit up. "How wonderful! I always wanted to do something like that when I was young, but never had the opportunity. I admire you for taking the chance to do it. But . . . what about your family? How do they feel? My husband would never have dreamed of letting me do something like that."

A lightning bolt of pain pierced her heart, but she pushed it away before it had time to force the tears to her eyes. "My . . . husband died a couple of years ago," she explained. "And my children are both away at college, so . . ."

Her voice drifted off, and she found herself at a loss to complete her thought. Mona jumped in and rescued her.

"Well, then, of course you can do something like this. It's the perfect time." She sighed. "If I were twenty years younger . . ." She paused and cast a slight glance in her husband's direction, but he was still glued to the cloud-filled scene outside the window. "If I were twenty years younger and didn't have anything or anyone holding me back, I'd find a way to go with you."

Julia smiled. The woman's words eased the churning in her stomach that had accompanied her since before she'd set foot on the plane. It was just the encouragement she needed to press on through the remainder of the long day ahead.

★ CHAPTER 5 ★

MARIE HAD WATCHED John go off to work after dropping Julia at the airport that morning as if nothing had changed, as if their only child hadn't just boarded a plane and flown off to a primitive, dangerous place where she would live for almost a year. Marie shivered at the thought. *Best-case scenario—she'll actually live through the school year and come home safely at the end of it.*

As the afternoon progressed, she scolded herself for her lack of faith, even as she mixed the ingredients for the meat loaf for that evening's dinner. She knew she should be praying instead of fussing and fuming, but she'd already prayed for weeks that Julia would change her mind and not go. What good had it done?

Marie shook her head as she shifted the mixture from the bowl to the baking pan, using her bare hands to pat it into a loaf shape. Why was it that everyone else who claimed to be so upset about Julia's foolish venture had gone on with their lives, while she stayed home and stewed? Tyler and Brittney were back at school, and John had abandoned her to go to work, even though he knew Marie wanted him to stay home and he could easily have done so.

"It's not like you're not old enough to retire," she huffed, punching the raw meat mixture into place. "You've been talking about it for five years, but every time you bring it up to your boss, you let him talk you out of it. Do you really think you're indispensable, that they can't get along without you? You're a good construction foreman, but you're not the only one. And even if you're not ready to retire yet, you could certainly take a few more days off now and then."

She sighed as she finished her task and washed her hands in hot water. She had to face facts. She'd seen John take days off for golf tournaments more than once, but when she needed him to stay home and give her moral support? Not even a consideration.

"Stop feeling sorry for yourself," she ordered, wiping her hands on the towel and opening the oven door. "You're pathetic." She slid the meat loaf inside, shut the door, and set the timer. Though she recognized the need to break out of her self-pity and do something useful while she waited to hear that Julia had arrived safely, she couldn't think of one thing that interested her enough to even try.

The thought of her friend Ginny Morales floated into her consciousness. Ginny was a good friend, someone who had been there for her through the years and was continually telling her she needed to get more involved in church activities and start volunteering her time. Marie closed her eyes and imagined Ginny giving one of her many pep talks. "Just because your kids and grandkids are grown doesn't mean you have to sit home in a rocker and knit. For heaven's sake, Marie, there are so many needs out there that you could fill. Get involved, girlfriend!"

Marie smiled in spite of her negative mood. Maybe Ginny was right. Maybe she did need to blast herself out of this house and find something useful to occupy her time. Wasn't that what she was always encouraging Julia to do—before she decided to run off to the middle of nowhere, that is?

The reminder drove away all thoughts of calling Ginny and finding out how best she could help at church or maybe even at the homeless shelter where Ginny spent so much of her time. Maybe she'd do that later; for now she would stay put and wait to hear from Julia.

★ ★ ★

HERNANDO WASN'T HAPPY. That meant everyone around him wasn't happy either. It was tough enough being banished to an area with little drug or gang activity, where he was supposed to find ways to cultivate income for his *jefe*, but in the rain forest? How could his boss expect him to live in such a place? Sure, he and his four *compadres* (close friends) had a semidecent *casita* (small house) in San Cristobal de las Casas, but so what? They were under strict orders to lay low except to snoop around for the rich tourists who occasionally frequented the area, and then find a way to kidnap some of them and extract ransom from their families. What kind of assignment was that for someone like him?

Nearly thirty years old, Hernando had been a successful, up-and-coming drug lord in Guadalajara before his assistant had messed up badly, causing the death of several of their gang members and the loss of more than a hundred thousand American dollars. That's when Hernando and three of the others had been demoted and sent to Chiapas State. Hernando had tried to argue that it was his assistant, Adolfo, who had caused the loss of life and money—not him. But his jefe didn't want to hear it. Adolfo had since met with a fatal accident, but apparently that wasn't enough. Ultimately Hernando realized he was lucky to walk away with his life and another chance to prove himself, even if it was far away from the women and nightlife that he had so enjoyed in Guadalajara.

He sat outside on the back porch, enjoying the late afternoon sun and swatting at a persistent fly. The others were taking their siesta inside. Later that evening they would split up and wander through the tourist areas of San Cristobal, seeking possible prey. They'd been here more than a week now and hadn't found anyone yet. Hernando was thinking they might need to head for San Juan Chamula. Though the town was smaller and the tourists fewer, they would be easier to spot and isolate—and, if all went well, easier to abduct. But he had to be sure first. He didn't dare mess up again and grab someone whose family couldn't produce the ransom. The last mistake had been deadly.

He had listened too much to Adolfo, who had recommended they kidnap a man Adolfo was certain had rich relatives. But as it turned out, not only did he not have wealthy family members, he was an undercover agent. The next thing the gang knew, gunfire seemed to erupt out of nowhere. The undercover agent was dirty and had brought in others like him, who murdered anyone who got in their way and stole the money they found in Hernando's home. It was a disaster, and Hernando knew he would not survive another such mistake.

The fly landed on his whiskered cheek, and this time Hernando didn't even bother to shoo it away. Instead he twitched his thick mustache, but the fly ignored it. Hernando cursed the heat and humidity that still hung on in the late summer afternoons but would soon disappear in the cooler temperatures of autumn.

★ ★ ★

JULIA THOUGHT THE DAY would never end. She had endured the first half of her journey into Angel Albino Corzo International Airport in Tuxtla Gutierrez, managed to board her connecting flight to Copalar Airport in Comitan, and was now nearing the end of that final leg of her air journey. *As rickety as this puddle jumper is, I hope they can land it safely.*

At last the plane was on the ground. Exhausted but grateful to have made it safely this far, she deplaned onto the tarmac and managed to locate her luggage. *Now if I can just find the Barneses. They said they'd be here.*

She stood in front of the relatively small airport, trying to appear more confident than she felt, wishing she had remembered to ask what sort of car they would be driving. The level of heat and humidity surprised her, as she had imagined it would cool off a bit more now that the sun was nearly down. Beginning to feel uncomfortable, she glanced around for a place to sit and wait. She had just spotted an empty bench when she heard a horn honk and someone call her name.

"Julia! Julia, over here!"

She turned to see a very old, very beat up, once-blue Jeep pull up and stop just in front of her. A familiar round face, framed with short gray curls, smiled at her from the open window.

"Sorry we're late," Carolyn explained, opening the door and climbing out as her husband did the same on the driver's side. "Nothing ever seems to run on time around here—including planes. Looks like yours was pretty much on schedule."

Before Julia could respond, Carolyn Barnes had pulled her into a warm hug, patting her back and kissing her on the cheek. "We're so glad you're here." She laughed. "I can't begin to tell you just *how* glad!"

Frank, who had come around the back of the Jeep, joined them. "Now, Carolyn, don't scare her off before we even get her home. Let her ease into this a bit, will you?"

Carolyn laughed again and Frank, who stood nearly a foot taller than both his wife and Julia, joined her as he added his own welcoming embrace. Julia laughed with them, hoping they didn't hear the nervous note in her voice.

In moments they had piled Julia's luggage in the back, and Julia found herself sitting up front with Frank. "I insist," Carolyn had said when Julia protested, explaining she could sit in the back. "You can see better up there. We want you to enjoy the scenery." Carolyn chuckled again. "Though it's nearly dark, so you may not see much. It's not like we have many street lights between here and home."

Julia did her best to peer through the near darkness and take in the sights as they drove along, the road getting bumpier by the mile. Before long she gave up and concentrated on holding on for dear life, praying she wouldn't knock herself out when her head hit the roof—which happened with alarming regularity.

It wasn't the first time and most certainly would not be the last that Julia Lawson Bennington would ask herself, *What in the world have I gotten myself into?*

★ CHAPTER 6 ★

BRITTNEY LOVED FALL. It seemed everywhere she looked she was engulfed in a brilliant profusion of rich colors—reds, gold, browns. Even her red-gold curls blended in. Yet this year wasn't the same. Though she did her best to throw herself into her studies and extracurricular activities, she struggled to concentrate.

Mom, you've been gone two weeks now. What are you doing today? Are you enjoying yourself? Are you safe?

She scuffed a small pile of fallen leaves as she trudged across the campus to her next class. The autumn sun was warm overhead but she scarcely felt it. Since voicing her thoughts regarding her mom's trip and despite the fact that she knew she had been right to do so, she'd had serious second thoughts. Why hadn't she simply kept those thoughts to herself instead of sharing them with her brother and grandparents? Tyler certainly hadn't agreed with her, and even her grandmother had looked at her in what appeared to be dismay at her betrayal. But her grandfather's solemn gaze and curt nod confirmed that she was right. None of them had heartily endorsed her mother's trip at that point, but at least John Lawson had eased off on his campaign to stop it.

Was I wrong? Brittney shifted her backpack from one shoulder to the other as she neared the doorway to her classroom. She knew her mom had arrived safely, as she'd emailed that information to them during one of the rare times the compound had Internet service. But they'd had no word since then. And that's what bothered her the most—the inability to communicate with her mother regularly.

Please take care of her, God, Brittney prayed silently as she pulled the door open and stepped inside. She realized then that ever since her mother had announced her intentions of going to Mexico, praying had once again become a regular part of her life.

Maybe that's a good thing, she thought, as she shrugged out of her backpack and took her seat. *I just hope it makes a difference.*

★ ★ ★

JULIA THOUGHT SHE'D never seen anything so lovely. True, the surrounding countryside, especially the rain forest, was breathtaking. But it was the children's faces—some glowing with excitement and anticipation, some closed off with shyness and mistrust, but all young and impressionable—that qualified as the loveliest sight of all.

She'd been teaching for nearly two weeks now, almost since the moment her feet hit the ground at La Paz Compound. Her hosts had graciously allowed her to unpack and retire early the first night, but after that it had been a sort of "baptism by fire" as she was thrust into the classroom the very next morning.

The challenges had been immediate and complicated. Her students consisted of eleven children, between the ages of six and eleven, five of which were boys and six girls. All spoke Spanish better than she, but she quickly found herself becoming more fluent by the day.

She smiled now, as she stood in front of her eleven charges, heads bent over their papers as they worked on their mathematics test. She'd always said she was more comfortable with older students and didn't feel qualified to teach the younger grades. It had never occurred to her that she might one day teach not only at an elementary level, but with students who varied in age by five years and who struggled to learn English as a second language.

Her glance fell on the one Mayan child who populated her classroom. Itzel, whose name meant "rainbow goddess," was one of the shy ones, possibly because even her Spanish was somewhat different from that of the other students due to the influence of her Mayan ancestry. *For her, English might almost be considered a third language,* Julia thought. More than once she'd caught herself eyeing the sweet-faced seven-year-old and wondering why her family even allowed her to come to their school. Most of the Mayans who wished to preserve what was left of their culture refused to have anything to do with the mission or its teachings.

The timer on her desk alerted them all that testing time was over. Julia watched as the children looked up and folded their papers, ready to pass them forward. It was easy to isolate the students who were confident of their answers, as they smiled when she caught their eyes. Others looked a bit distressed but obediently laid their pencils down. Itzel, on the other hand, while following directions to stop writing and turn in her paper, did so without looking up. Julia could count on one hand the times she'd actually been able to make eye contact with the child.

You've only been here two weeks, she reminded herself. *Give her time. She'll come around.* Then she marveled at the fact that connecting with Itzel mattered to her so quickly.

All the students. I want to connect with all the students and to help them whatever way I can—though I sometimes wonder at the wisdom or necessity of teaching them English.

She sighed as she collected the papers from the students sitting in the front desks. Itzel, though smaller and younger than most of the children, refused to sit toward the front of the room.

It's not just me she shies away from; it's the other students too. She must be very lonely here.

"Señora Bennington?"

The soft voice interrupted Julia's thoughts as she placed the collected tests on her desk. Turning back toward her students she spotted Marina, a pleasant ten-year old and the youngest child of the compound's pastor, Ramon Perez, with her hand in the air.

Julia smiled at her and purposely answered in English. "Yes, Marina? What is it?"

The girl struggled, speaking slowly, but obviously determined to answer in her second language. "We have . . . housework . . .?" She paused, frowning before shaking her head and continuing. "No. Homework. We have homework today?"

Julia nodded, pleased at the girl's progress. "Yes, Marina, we do." Slowly, in English, she explained the evening's assignment, then repeated it in Spanish to be sure everyone understood before dismissing them for the day.

"*Gracias,* Señora Bennington!"

"*Adios, señora!*"

Excited children, knowing they were excused to enjoy the compound's playground for nearly an hour before their parents or other guardians came to pick them up, reverted to Spanish as they scrambled into line by the door, waiting patiently until Julia opened it and let them out.

Her eyes followed them. Some skipped or ran, while others walked in pairs or groups, excitedly chattering with their companions. Only Itzel trailed along behind, head bowed, as she made her way to her usual spot on the bench overlooking the playground. Despite Julia's encouragement to join in with the others, Itzel kept to herself until her grandmother came to get her. Then, silently, the two made their way down the dirt pathway from the campground.

The grandmother is even more closed-mouthed than Itzel. I just can't imagine why the girl is allowed to come here.

She shrugged and sighed. There were tests to grade and lessons to prepare. Perhaps she'd take the tests out to the playground and sit on the bench with Itzel, grading them there even if the girl didn't speak to her or look her way. For now, the important thing was to help the child feel comfortable in her presence. Developing a relationship would have to come later.

★ ★ ★

"**Perdona, señora,** but I saw you sitting with Itzel today. Did she speak to you?"

Julia looked up from where she sat in her chair behind her desk. The children, including Itzel, had gone home, and she'd returned to her classroom to finish the last of her work before heading back to her little cottage next door to the Barneses.

Padre Ramon stood in the open doorway, a hesitant smile on his face. In the two weeks since arriving at the compound, Julia had come to like this humble, kind man, though she couldn't help but notice the sadness is his dark eyes. Just a few inches taller than her own five-foot-two-inch frame, he had a slight build and yet walked with a strength that she knew came from within.

She smiled in return. "I'm afraid not, Padre. I've tried, but I doubt I've been able to elicit more than a half dozen words from her since I arrived here. And those were all in Spanish, not English. Still, from the way she follows directions, regardless of which language I use, I think she understands at least some English. Am I right?"

The man with thick, wavy salt-and-pepper hair stepped into the room, hesitating until she invited him the rest of the way by indicating the empty chair beside her desk.

"Gracias," he said, taking a seat. "I believe you are right, though I too have heard her speak very little during the past months since she's been coming here."

"So she's a fairly new student."

Ramon nodded. "*Sí,* less than one year. Her *abuela* (grandmother) showed up with her one day and asked if she could come to school here. The Barneses said yes, and the old woman has been bringing her and picking her up ever since." He shrugged. "The *viejita* hasn't spoken to us since that first day. I wanted to try to find where they live and see if I could speak with the abuela or someone else in the family, but the

Barneses asked me not to. They thought it might scare them off completely. Itzel is the only Mayan student we have here. The others avoid us—or worse."

Julia swallowed. She'd already heard horror stories of people disappearing at the hands of some of the curanderos, or shamans, in the area, the worst story being that of Ramon's own wife. Though she understood he couldn't prove that his beloved Rosa had died at the hands of some of the more aggressive or resentful Mayans, it was generally assumed that it had been so. She admired the man's ability not to hold a grudge or become bitter.

Changing the subject, she smiled. "Marina is a very good student. You must be very proud of her."

Ramon's smile was quick and full, bringing out tiny wrinkles around his eyes. Her impression of the man as being humble and kind deepened at that moment. "Sí, señora, I am very proud of all my children. But Marina is my baby, the one most like her mother."

A hint of sadness flitted across his face, and he dropped his eyes.

Julia resisted the impulse to lay a comforting hand on his, knowing it would be inappropriate. Instead she said, "You still miss her very much, don't you?"

When he lifted his gaze, tears glistened in his eyes. He nodded. "Sí, señora. But I know she is safe with our Lord. And that helps me very much."

A bolt of jagged lightning seemed to slice through her heart, as she fought to keep from saying something she would regret. She knew what it was like to miss a beloved spouse, but she couldn't relate to the rest of his statement so she would once again change the subject.

"Well," she said, gathering together her papers and books before standing to her feet, "it's getting late. I'd better get going."

Ramon rose from his chair. "Will we see you at the service this evening?"

Julia blanched. She'd forgotten about the midweek service that everyone else in the compound attended each Wednesday evening. The Barneses had invited her the last two weeks, not only on Wednesday but Sunday mornings too, and would no doubt do the same tonight. She'd been able to plead weariness until now, but she knew that wouldn't hold much longer.

She smiled. "We'll see. Good night, Padre."

Before he could press her further, she swept past him and out the door.

★ CHAPTER 7 ★

JULIA KNEW WHO STOOD at her front door, knocking, before she opened it. She'd made the short walk across the compound from the school to her cottage more than an hour earlier, determined to put the padre's invitation out of her mind. Hoping for an Internet connection, she'd spent the next hour trying to send emails to her parents and children, but to no avail. The compound had been quiet, and though she'd never been one to take naps, she found herself growing drowsy as she sat on her tiny patio and tried to read. Within moments she had dozed off.

But now the afternoon sunlight was gone, and she was hungry. She'd prepared a sandwich and fruit in her kitchen and then sat down in the armchair beside her bed to work on the next day's lessons. That's when the knock had come. Julia glanced at her watch and realized it had to be Frank and Carolyn Barnes on their way to the evening service. No doubt they had stopped by to try to convince her to join them.

She greeted them now, these two dear people whom she so admired and who now stood gazing at her with smiling faces and hopeful eyes. "We came to invite you to join us at church," Carolyn offered. "The service starts in a few minutes."

Julia opened her mouth to decline their invitation, hoping to excuse herself by explaining she had lessons to prepare. But she knew how weak and transparent her excuse would sound. She'd had all afternoon to work on the lessons, and there truly wasn't that much to prepare in the first place.

She offered a thin-lipped smile. "Sure. Just let me grab a light shawl. I noticed it got a bit cool when I was sitting outside last night after the sun went down."

"Absolutely," Carolyn agreed. "This time of year the temperature drops quickly after dark."

Within moments the three of them were walking the hundred yards or so from Julia's place to the church building, a small one-room edifice with a thatched roof and the words *La Iglesia de la Paz*—the Church of Peace—handpainted over the front door. Padre Ramon's living quarters were attached at the back. Frank Barnes walked silently to his wife's left, while Carolyn chatted nearly nonstop, her arm linked in Julia's.

"I'm so glad you decided to come," she said. "It will give you a chance to meet the locals who come to our services. There aren't many, but we're growing. Padre Ramon is such a godly man, and we have all benefited from his teaching and leadership."

Julia nodded. She hadn't heard the man's teachings yet, but she didn't doubt that he was indeed a godly man, though she sometimes wondered exactly what such a definition entailed. But her few brief meetings with him since arriving at La Paz assured her that he was sincere.

Sounds of singing in Spanish, combined with an accompanying guitar, greeted them as they approached. Once inside Julia saw that it was Padre Ramon himself who sat on a tall, three-legged stool at the front, strumming his guitar and leading the fifteen or twenty parishioners in song. His simple white cotton shirt and pants were the same he'd worn when she'd seen him earlier. *He dresses like his flock—simple and unassuming. I like that.*

Ramon glanced up and caught her eye as she and the Barneses settled into folding chairs toward the back of the room. A slight smile and nod confirmed that he'd seen them. She returned the smile as he glanced back down at his guitar and continued to sing.

Not the best voice in the world, she thought, *but pleasant and gentle—like him.*

As much as she was able with songs she'd not heard before, she joined in singing with the others.

IT WAS THURSDAY MORNING, and Hernando was encouraged. They'd spotted a tourist couple who seemed to be loners, always breaking away from the tour-bus crowd. Best of all, he and his compadres had watched them closely all morning and concluded they had money, as they flashed it around each time they made a purchase. That meant they most likely had family at home who would be willing and able to pull together a decent ransom to have them set free. All Hernando and his cohorts had to do was find a way to kidnap and whisk them away without being caught.

The four men broke up into pairs, taking turns keeping an eye on the couple. By evening they knew exactly what hotel they were in, including which room. Once the tour group was safely settled in for the night, the men would make their move. If all went well, the unsuspecting middle-aged couple would soon be hidden away in a safe place, their lives dependent on their loved ones meeting their kidnappers' demands.

Hernando grinned as he watched the sun begin its descent toward the area's many mountains and trees. The tourist group was out celebrating at a local *cantina* this evening; by morning they would be astonished to learn that two of their number had disappeared. The thought excited him. And didn't he deserve a little excitement in his life? He was used to the bright lights and exotic nightlife of the big city, but he'd been banished to the middle of nowhere. Not only did he have to prove himself to those in charge, he also had to make his own entertainment as well. It appeared he would soon be successful at both.

★ ★ ★

"SEÑORA BENNINGTON?"

The familiar voice stopped Julia as she left the school building on Thursday afternoon, heading for home.

She turned to see Padre Ramon's daughter, Marina, trailing behind her.

"Hello, Marina," she said, stopping to wait for the girl. "Do you need something?"

Marina's delicate features took on a hesitant appearance as she slowed her steps. She nodded, her long black braids hanging thickly over the back of her shoulders. Her dark eyes were round and clear.

"Yo quiero . . ." She began in Spanish but quickly switched to English. "I want to know if . . . if I am doing well in my studies. My brother and sister will be coming home to visit soon, and I want them to be proud of me."

Julia's heart melted. She hadn't yet met Padre Ramon's two older children, twins named Cristina and Antonio. They were quite a bit older than their little sister and had been sent to live with relatives in Mexico City, where they were attending their first year of college. Julia admired their father's tenacity at making sure his children got whatever education possible to give them a chance at a better future, but right now she was touched by Ramon's youngest child's desire to please her older siblings.

"You are doing very well, Marina. Your work is some of the best in the class. Your brother and sister will be very proud of you." She smiled and laid a hand on the girl's shoulder. "I am proud of you too."

Marina's face lit up, all vestiges of hesitation having vanished. "You are?" She stepped forward and threw her arms around Julia's waist. "Oh, gracias, Señora Bennington! Gracias."

Overwhelmed by the child's impulsive display of gratitude, Julia found herself at a loss for words as unbidden tears stung her eyes. Another thread wove itself around her heart, deepening her connection to the people of La Paz.

★ CHAPTER 8 ★

THE TERRIFIED PAIR SAT STIFFLY, blindfolded, bound, and gagged, back-to-back in hard wooden chairs. Darkness enveloped them, and they had no way of knowing if it was day or night. It was exactly as Hernando had planned it.

The woman moaned, and Hernando watched her, imagining she had once been attractive, but no more. Too many years and too much rich life had taken their toll. It was too bad. He would have liked to enjoy himself with her for a while before releasing her—or killing her, if the ransom didn't arrive.

Her moaning and whimpering, though muffled through her gag, continued, causing Bruno the pit bull to growl in response. The dog was trained to guard whatever prey it was assigned, in this case the kidnapped tourists. Hernando trusted Bruno to a point but wouldn't want to turn his back on the beast. He imagined his captives were nearly as terrified of the animal as they were of their situation in general.

Snatching them from their motel room had been a walk in the park. The gang members had silently jimmied the lock on their door, slipped inside, and gagged them before they could make a sound. Now, more than twenty-four hours later, they understood they were being held for ransom. Though they'd argued that their families in Canada didn't have the kind of money the men were demanding, Hernando had made it clear that they'd better hope their families found a way to come up with it if they wanted to get out alive.

A synchronized rap on the door brought Bruno to full attention. The growls resumed as he awaited direction.

Hernando recognized the signal and opened the door.

"I brought breakfast," the man said, handing Hernando a thermos of coffee and several large burritos. "You ready for a break?"

Technically it was still Hernando's shift for another hour, but since his compadre had offered, he decided to take him up on it.

"Sure." He took the food and motioned with his head for the man to come inside. "They slept a little, but not much. The woman cries a lot, but otherwise everything is quiet. Let's give them a quick break to relieve themselves and eat something while we're both here. Then we'll tie them back up and I'll go back to the house for a few minutes."

With four of them plus Bruno to guard their captives, Hernando wasn't at all concerned about the couple making an escape. The house was mere steps away from the old outbuilding where they were being held, and even that was well hidden among the trees in the backyard. One of them stayed with the couple at all times.

He set the food down and helped his partner untie the pair. He figured they'd be back in their chairs in fifteen minutes, tops, and then he could eat his own breakfast and get some sleep. He'd be glad when this business was finished. He just hoped it ended well, with the man and his wife on their way home and a big chunk of money in the gang's possession. There was an alternate plan, of course, but it certainly wasn't one that any of them preferred.

★ ★ ★

SATURDAY MORNING DAWNED DAMP AND GRAY, with a heavy fog lying over the compound and as far out into the forest as Julia could see. She'd grown accustomed to having her morning coffee on her little patio, enjoying the sun and listening to the forest come to life. But today was too cold. With no classes in the offing, she sat in the comfortable armchair beside her bed, wrapped in a blanket and ingesting her caffeine. One thing she'd learned about Mexican coffee— it was hot, black, and strong, and it was starting to grow on her. She'd have a difficult time readjusting to frothy lattes and cappuccinos when she went back home.

Home. I've only been gone a few weeks, but it seems longer. It's like being transported into a different world—certainly a different time. Since being here I've been able to access the Internet and check email exactly five times, and that only briefly, I haven't a clue what's going on in the rest of the world.

She smiled, hugging her cup between her hands. *Maybe that's not such a bad thing. Working with the children keeps me busy, and I enjoy the overall slower pace, even if much of what we do and experience here seems so primitive. But is that such a bad thing?*

Her mind wandered to Marina, no doubt her star pupil. The child was not only eager to learn but also to please. She had a quick mind and a humble heart, as well as a lovely face. How could anyone not love her?

The thought that she'd had to spend much of her childhood without a mother tugged at Julia's heartstrings. All three of Padre Ramon's children had lost their mother, but the older two had her much longer than little Marina.

Her thoughts turned then to her own children. Tyler and Brittney still missed their father dearly, but like the padre's two older children, they hadn't been little when he died. Julia couldn't imagine not having her own parents there for her throughout her earliest years.

Mom and Dad. The two of you can be more than a little interfering at times, but I never doubted that you loved me. Something tells me Padre Ramon's children have that same confidence in their father as well.

The occasional call of a monkey, somewhere out in the treetops, suddenly turned to a cacophony of cries, and Julia peered out her window. She could see nothing of the nearby animals but imagined they were embroiled in some sort of squabble over food or pecking rights.

As suddenly as the argument had started, it stopped. The sounds of the forest were beginning to seem normal to Julia, though the strange noises during her first few nights in the compound had caused her to wonder if she'd ever get a good night's sleep in the place.

She'd stopped worrying about that now. Not only had she begun to sleep peacefully through the night, but she was adapting to regular afternoon siestas as well, at least on the days when she wasn't teaching. On school days she spent that after lunch time working on papers and trying to interact with the children, who played jump rope and other simple outdoor games.

Taking another sip of coffee, she realized she couldn't remember when she'd last felt so rested.

★ ★ ★

THE DOORBELL RANG, pulling Marie away from the ironing she was doing in her sunny kitchen. She frowned. John had left more than an hour earlier to play his usual Saturday morning round of golf, and Marie wasn't expecting anyone.

She placed the iron upright on the board and headed for the front door. Her heart warmed and she smiled when she pulled the door open and found her friend Ginny Morales standing on the front porch.

"Ginny, what a nice surprise!" She ushered her inside, taking her blue windbreaker from her in the process. "What's up? Did I forget something?"

Ginny smiled, her brown eyes warm and surrounded with laugh lines. "Not a thing. I know I should have called first, but I was on my way to the church for a meeting about the homeless ministry and decided it couldn't hurt to stop by and invite you to go with me—again."

Marie felt the objections rising up inside her. "Oh, I couldn't," she said, shaking her head. "I have so many things to do today. In fact, I was just ironing when you stopped by."

Ginny parked her hands on her ample hips and shook her head. "Marie Lawson, that's exactly why I didn't call first. I knew you'd have an excuse; you always do. But that ironing can wait, and you know it. The meeting only lasts an hour or so, and then we can go out for a nice cup of coffee and a visit. You'll be back here by noon."

Marie felt her resolve start to melt, but she shook the feeling away. "I can't, Ginny. Really. John will be home by eleven, and I always have something ready for him to eat when he gets here."

Ginny's eyes narrowed. "And you can't just leave him a sandwich?"

Marie knew she could, but she shook her head. "He wouldn't know where I was. I can't call him on his cell while he's on the golf course because he turns it off while he's playing, and I don't want him to worry if he comes home and I'm not here."

Ginny rolled her eyes. "So you leave him a message."

"He hardly ever thinks to check them."

"So leave him a nice big note, right next to his sandwich, on the kitchen table. He can read, right?"

A giggle began to work its way up from somewhere deep inside. Marie swallowed it but allowed a smile to pop out. "You're right," she conceded at last. "Maybe getting out for a while this morning is exactly what I need. And to be honest, John is always telling me to get involved more at church." She hesitated. "I have to be honest, though. I don't know yet whether or not I want to be involved in the homeless ministry."

"Of course you don't." Ginny's warm smile was back. "You don't have to commit or decide anything today. Just come to the meeting, find out what we're doing and how you can help, and then pray about it. That's it. No pressure."

After a final moment of hesitation, Marie gave a quick nod. "All right. Let's do it. I just need to go shut off the iron, make John a quick sandwich, and write that note. Give me five minutes."

"You've got 'em. And I'll help, so we just might get out of here even sooner than that."

They laughed, and Marie led the way back to the kitchen, both pleased and surprised at the sense of anticipation she felt.

★ CHAPTER 9 ★

JULIA'S QUIET SATURDAY MORNING had been interrupted when Carolyn Barnes knocked at her door and asked, "How about riding into San Cristobal with Frank and me to pick up some supplies?"

Julia had readily accepted the offer and thoroughly enjoyed the outing. Unlike her initial trip from the airport to the compound, it hadn't been dark so she was able to enjoy the lush, even primitive, scenery. Much of the forested and mountainous countryside appeared to have been untouched by humanity or time, but that preserved beauty contrasted sharply with the noise and glitter of San Cristobal's downtown area. Still, she had enjoyed escaping the confines of La Paz and getting a better feel for the surrounding countryside.

After they returned and the supplies were unloaded and stowed, Julia had asked about the rain forest itself. "It's so lovely from here—what I can see of it. Is it possible to go exploring?"

Both Fred and Carolyn had cautioned her about doing so alone but had also offered to take her on a brief excursion themselves. Now, highlighted by the temperate afternoon sunshine, the three ventured into the thick stands of trees. Within seconds they found themselves in heavy foliage that the sunlight struggled to penetrate.

"This is so beautiful," Julia breathed, somehow feeling the need to speak softly. "And so peaceful! It's as if it has never been touched by human hands."

Frank, who led the way, paused and turned to Julia. The three of them stood still as he spoke. "It may seem that way, but in most areas that's not true. Some spots in the Lacandon Jungle have been stripped nearly bare, but it's still

A CHRISTMAS GIFT

the largest rain forest in North America." He leaned forward slightly. "Also one of the few places left in the world that contains jaguars."

Julia felt her eyes widen and the hair rise on the back of her neck. "I . . . I've heard strange sounds a couple of times, and I didn't think it was monkeys or birds. It sounded more like a growl or cry from a large cat."

Frank nodded. "That's probably exactly what you've heard. We've never actually spotted one, probably because they don't tend to come near the compound, but there's little doubt they're out here."

Carolyn laid a hand on Julia's arm. "They seldom approach humans," she said, her voice soothing, "but their presence is one of several reasons we advise people never to come out here alone." A hint of tears popped into Carolyn's dark eyes, but she quickly blinked them away. "You know, that's what happened to Ramon's poor wife. She came out here alone and . . . never came back. I told you about that, didn't I?"

Julia nodded. Carolyn had indeed told her, but it seemed likely the woman had died as a result of human foul play, not an attack from a wild animal. Tragic.

Frank turned away, and he and Carolyn resumed their trek deeper into the trees, pushing away branches and vines as they walked. Julia followed close behind, noticing the ruckus they stirred up with the monkeys hiding in the branches overhead. She liked to think they were welcoming them, but she doubted it.

Once again Frank stopped, as did Carolyn and then Julia. "I'm sure you already know this area is a stronghold of Mayan culture and belief, though much has been mixed with Spanish culture and the Catholic faith. As a result, superstition runs rampant and many of the Mayan descendants are leery of what they consider interlopers. Understandably so, of course. The Spanish nearly wiped out the Mayan way of life when they arrived here, and those of

Mayan ancestry who wish to cling to their ancient ways have a deep-seated resentment toward outsiders." He smiled. "That would be us, of course."

Julia's mind flashed back to the many sights she'd seen earlier that day. "I noticed an old woman walking down the street in town. She stood out because she was wearing such varied and brilliant colors. I also noticed a piece of glass hanging from a chain around her neck. I spotted it when it glinted in the sun. I meant to ask you about it. I don't know why, but I got a strange feeling when she happened to glance my way."

"I'm not surprised," Frank answered. "I didn't notice her, but she was no doubt a shaman. There are many in the area, and they're often called curanderos or curanderas. Both men and women, they're more or less the Mayans' version of a witch doctor, and they're highly respected among their people. The piece of glass you saw was really a small mirror. The curanderos wear them to ward off evil spirits." He paused and shook his head. "What they don't realize is that they themselves are dealing with evil spirits when they practice their occult faith."

For the second time in minutes, Julia's hair rose on the back of her neck. She knew her parents would understand Frank's talk of witch doctors and evil spirits and would certainly agree that the local shamans were engaged in the occult. For herself, however, Julia wasn't sure how she felt about such things. It was difficult to believe in something that seemed so outdated. And yet . . . hadn't she virtually left the twenty-first century behind and willingly come to dwell in a place that had scarcely made connection with the twentieth century?

She pushed those thoughts to the back of her mind, determined not to let such superstitious nonsense ruin her enjoyment of the beauty of this tranquil place. She loved it here and looked forward to venturing out into this magnificent greenery as often as possible.

RAMON HAD NOTICED the Barneses and Julia head out in the Jeep earlier that day and later, after they returned, he saw them slip outside the compound in the direction of the forest. Ramon told himself it was only natural that the woman from the United States wanted to explore her new environment, and he knew the best way to do that was in the company of those who had already become accustomed to it. Fred and Carolyn Barnes had been here long enough now to appreciate the area's beauty as well as its dangers, and he knew they would look out for Julia in her inexperience. Still, the loss of his beloved *esposa* was too fresh to brush away the uneasiness he felt when someone naively entered the forest.

Julia had quickly endeared herself to the Barneses and Ramon, as well as the students who came and went daily. Ramon told himself his reason for feeling such an immediate connection to the woman was because she was so good with the children, particularly Marina, who obviously adored her. *Perhaps that is part of it—most of it,* Ramon reasoned. *But I am concerned that I care for her too because she is a woman . . . an attractive one.* He shook his head, a sense of guilt washing over him. *I have no right. And why would such an educated and sophisticated woman even notice me? I am a foolish, arrogant man. Forgive me, Lord . . .*

With Julia and the Barneses still outside the compound exploring the rain forest, Ramon forced himself to walk into the chapel and into a tiny cubicle off the back that served as a makeshift office. Tomorrow was Sunday; he had a sermon to finish.

He sat at his rough-hewn desk and opened his Bible. "Open my ears and my heart, Lord," he whispered. "Let me hear Your voice and know what You want me to speak to Your people tomorrow. Wipe away my arrogance, Father, so that I might speak humbly and clearly. And please prepare the hearts of those You bring here to listen tomorrow morning. Only You know their hearts, Lord, not I. I have no qualifications to stand before them, but I believe You have called me to do so, and so I must obey. Honor my obedience, *El Señor*, for it is all I have to offer."

It is enough.

The answer came softly, but it drowned out his insecurities and doubts as he began to read from the Book he so dearly loved.

★ CHAPTER 10 ★

SUNDAY MORNING BROUGHT THE HOT, dry winds known as *Santa Anas,* or "devil winds," to Southern California. Brittney had planned to sleep in but awoke before 8:00, too restless to go back to sleep.

Better to get up and get some studying done anyway, she thought, yawning as she forced herself to a sitting position. *Major tests coming soon, might as well get started.*

She glanced across the room at her roommate, Chloe—still sleeping, and probably would be for the next few hours. The girl had been out late again, no doubt partying and definitely not studying. Brittney sat up, arched her back, stretched, then stuffed her feet into her scruffy slippers and headed to their shared closet to find some comfy clothes for the day.

Thirty minutes later she was showered and dressed in white, midcalf cotton pants and an off-the-shoulder baggy pink blouse. Her long red-gold hair hung damp and thick down her back and shoulders. She snatched her backpack full of books, stuffed her notebook into the front compartment, and headed for the door.

After a brief stop at the campus coffee shop for a large cappuccino, she headed straight for the library, imagining it would be mostly empty so early on a Sunday morning. Warm, dry wind gusts blew her curls as she crossed the large grassy area between the coffee shop and library. Her hair was nearly dry by the time she stepped through the double doors, but she could only imagine how wild and unkempt it must look. Determined to rein it in as best she could with the large hairclip she'd stuck in her backpack, she aimed for the women's restroom in the back.

"Britt?"

The familiar voice stopped her in her tracks. "Tyler?" She blinked in surprise at the sight of her big brother parked at a table just feet from the restroom entrance.

"What are you doing here?" they asked in unison, then broke into laughter.

The only other student in the room, a young Asian man with glasses, looked up and frowned in their direction. When they swallowed their laughter, he went back to his reading.

Brittney plunked down beside her brother. "Seriously, what are you doing here? You never get up this early, at least not on the weekends."

Tyler nodded. "I know. But I've really gotten behind on assignments lately. I need to get serious before I get in trouble." He cocked his head. "But hey, I'm not the only one who doesn't usually get up early. So why are you here—and what in the world happened to your hair? You look like you got struck by lightning."

Brittney reached up and tried in vain to smooth down her unruly locks. "I was headed for the restroom to do something with this mop when I saw you. And I'm here because I woke up early and thought I might as well hit the studies. I'm probably not as far behind as you, but I do have tests coming up."

"We all do." He shook his head. "College life is great, but it can be tough too."

"That's for sure. Here, you want a sip of my cappuccino?"

"I'd like more than a sip, but I'll settle for a gulp or two." He took the cup from her and drank what she was certain was nearly half of her morning caffeine.

"Hey, they do have a coffee shop here on campus, you know." She took the cup back from him. "And for a couple bucks, you can get one of these all for yourself."

He grinned. "I know. But it's a lot more fun to drink yours. Cheaper too."

She swatted at him, but he ducked. "Some things never change, do they, big brother?"

His grin faded. "Except with Mom. I've been thinking about her a lot this morning. Have you heard from her lately?"

"Just the couple of emails that she sent to both of us. I guess Internet access really is spotty there."

"Sounds like everything even close to civilized is spotty there. I still can't believe she did something so crazy. It's just not like her."

"True. But maybe that's exactly why she decided to do it."

Tyler frowned, his dark eyes glowering. "That's the other thing I can't believe in all this—why you supported her and encouraged her to do it."

"I did not encourage her, and you know it. I didn't want her to go any more than you did. But I just didn't think it was right for us to stand in her way for selfish reasons."

"Selfish reasons?" Tyler's voice rose. "Wanting to keep our mother alive and safe? In case you've forgotten, it hasn't been that long since Dad died."

Brittney held up her hand and shushed him. "Of course I haven't forgotten. But I still don't think we had the right to try to stop her if it's what she really wanted to do."

Tyler's voice returned to a whisper, but he nearly hissed as he talked. "So what if something happens to her? Will you still feel the same way?"

An arrow of fear pierced Brittney's heart, but she clenched her jaw and continued. "I hope and pray nothing happens to her and that she comes home safe and sound. That's all I can do. She's an adult, you know—and so are we. We need to act like it."

Tyler shook his head and turned away, waving his hand in the direction of the restroom. "Go fix your hair. You look like a wild woman."

Brittney felt her eyes narrow. She understood how Tyler felt, but she didn't appreciate his attitude. Biting back words that could only make things worse, she stood up from the table and headed for the restroom, her hair flying and bouncing behind her.

★ ★ ★

JULIA HAD SURVIVED THE WEEKEND, including attending the Sunday morning service with the Barneses. She'd come to the conclusion that it was easier to go with them on a regular basis than to try to come up with plausible excuses every Sunday morning and Wednesday evening. Besides, there wasn't that much else going on during those times, so she might as well become as much a part of the life of La Paz as possible.

She had to admit that she enjoyed the simple, humble words and messages of Padre Ramon. Each time she heard him speak to the congregation or spoke with him one-on-one, her respect for him grew. He was a good man with strong convictions and an uncompromising faith. He wasn't bad to look at either, in his own unpretentious way, but she pushed that thought away every time it tried to make inroads into her heart or mind.

Now it was Monday, and the school day was over. The children's playtime was drawing to a close, and as usual, Itzel sat on the bench, head bowed and silent. Though she knew it was probably pointless, Julia decided to make an effort to speak with the child.

"How are you, Itzel?" she asked in Spanish as she joined her on the bench.

The little girl didn't raise her head. *"Estoy bien,"* she mumbled, assuring her she was fine. Then she coughed.

It wasn't the first time Julia had heard her cough that day, and despite the child's reply that she was well, Julia wondered if it were true. Hesitantly she reached out her hand to touch the girl's forehead. It was hot.

Itzel drew back, glancing up only long enough for Julia to see the fear in her eyes.

"I'm sorry," Julia said, scooting closer but being careful not to touch her again. "I noticed you've been coughing today, and I think you might have a fever."

Itzel's head was once again bowed, her shoulder-length black hair hanging forward and covering her face. She didn't answer.

"Can I help?" Julia asked. "Would you like a glass of water? Or you can come to my cottage and lie down until your abuela gets here."

She shook her head.

Julia sighed. She supposed there was nothing she could do now except wait until the girl's grandmother showed up to walk her home.

In less than twenty minutes the old woman arrived. The moment Itzel heard her voice calling her name, she jumped up from the bench but swayed a moment before regaining her balance. Julia stood up and put an arm around her, holding her until the grandmother joined them.

"Come," the old woman ordered, ignoring Julia. "We go home."

Itzel tried to respond, taking a shaky step in her grandmother's direction. But Julia sensed the girl was still woozy.

"She's not feeling well," Julia said, hoping the old woman understood her not-quite-perfect Spanish. "Maybe we should let her lie down for a few minutes. Señora Barnes has nurse's training and can take a look at her."

The old woman's head jerked upward, and her dark eyes blazed. "No! No nurse. We go home. Now."

Julia swallowed and nodded. "All right. I hope she feels better soon."

She stepped back and watched as Itzel and her grandmother began to walk toward the main gate. It was obvious they were both struggling, as Itzel leaned against the old woman. As the gate opened to let them out, Julia made a heart decision that bypassed her mind. She ran to join them, stopping on the other side of Itzel and once again slipping her arm around the girl's waist, falling into step with them. The grandmother glanced at her briefly, but said nothing as the three of them made their way down the dirt road leading away from the compound.

★ ★ ★

MARIE LAWSON HADN'T FELT so invigorated in a very long time. She'd attended the homeless ministry meeting with her friend Ginny Morales on Saturday, gone to church with John on Sunday, and then spent Monday morning helping out at the homeless shelter. She hadn't had any direct contact with the residents at the ministry, but she'd devoted the first several hours of the day to cooking the biggest pots of vegetable soup she'd ever seen. Now, as she rode in the passenger seat of Ginny's car, she was tired but pleased.

"You enjoyed it, didn't you?"

Ginny's question drew her attention from her jumbled thoughts. She pulled her eyes from the window, where she'd been staring, unseeing, at the passing scenery.

"I did." She smiled. "I enjoyed it very much. I can't imagine why I waited so long to agree to help out."

Ginny nodded and returned Marie's smile. "I knew you would. I was the same way. I resisted every invitation to join that ministry until I just flat ran out of excuses. I finally decided to go—just once—so I could say I did, and I planned to make that the end of it." Her smiled widened. "I've been going every week since, and that was four years ago."

Marie chuckled. "I'm glad to hear I'm not the only one." She shook her head. "To be honest, I think the thing that held me back most was thinking I'd feel so guilty about how much I had when I saw those who had so little. But as it turned out, I scarcely caught sight of any of the people living there."

"And you won't for a while," Ginny explained. "We try to keep your direct involvement with the residents to a minimum at first—not so much for your sake as for theirs. They grow attached to us and consider us their friends. We want to be sure you're going to make a commitment to keep coming at least once a week before we introduce you to them."

"That makes sense." She sighed. "I can't even imagine how those people must feel, living in that shelter as they do."

Without taking her eyes from the road, Ginny reached over and patted Marie's hand. "They feel very fortunate because the shelter is so much better than the streets—and that's where most of them came from and where so many still live right now. We're only able to help such a small percentage of those who need us. But at least we help some."

Tears stung Marie's eyes. Since leaving the shelter minutes earlier, she'd wondered whether or not she'd commit to going again. At that moment she no longer wondered. In fact, she couldn't wait to return.

★ CHAPTER 11 ★

THE SMALL WOMAN IN THE EMBROIDERED RED BLOUSE, long black skirt, and black shawl draped over her shoulders trudged along quietly, with Itzel and Julia in tow. Julia made mental notes of all landmarks along the way, though so far they hadn't made any detours from the main road.

After about fifteen minutes they finally veered right, off the road and into a small gathering of low breeze-block buildings, most with thatched roofs. Chickens wandered and pecked at the ground at will, oblivious to the handful of malnourished dogs also prowling the area. Suspicious eyes peered from dark doorways as the three females passed by. Julia tried to offer a smile to the first of the observers, but gave up when a stone-faced response was all she got.

Without a word the old woman stopped in front of one of the smaller homes. "Gracias," she said, her head lifted defiantly as she glared at Julia.

Before Julia could answer, Itzel and her grandmother had disappeared inside the house and closed the door behind them. Julia thought about knocking, hoping to gain admittance, but she realized it would be a futile attempt. Sensing a darkness sweep over her, despite the bright sunshine overhead, she turned away and began the journey back toward La Paz, conscious of the many warnings she'd received about not being outside the compound alone. But what else could she have done? It was obvious Itzel wasn't well, and her grandmother didn't appear strong enough to get the girl home without help. Julia had done what she had to do, and now she had to get herself back—safely and quickly.

She picked up her pace, her face straight forward yet feeling the stares that seemed to bore into her back. She'd been told that strangers were not welcome here, and now she knew it firsthand. But if all strangers were viewed as dangerous and even evil, why did Itzel's grandmother continue to bring her to school every day? It certainly wasn't required, and the vast majority of the area's residents had nothing to do with anyone from La Paz.

The question haunted her all the way until the gates of the compound came into sight and she breathed a sigh of relief.

★ ★ ★

RAMON SPOTTED HER the minute she walked through the compound gates—alone. His heart raced at the implications. Where had she been? Did she realize how foolish it was to leave La Paz by herself?

Without taking time to think or pray, he intercepted Julia on her way to her cottage.

"Where were you?" he asked in Spanish. "Why did you go out alone?"

The look of surprise on her face quickly took on a tinge of annoyance as she stopped and faced him.

"Excuse me?"

She had answered in English, so Ramon did the same, already feeling some remorse at his confrontational attitude. "Forgive me, señora, but . . ." He paused and took a deep breath. "I should not have approached you in such a manner, but I was concerned. Surely the Barneses have warned you about going outside alone."

The woman's face softened, and Ramon found himself wondering how a woman in her late forties could still appear so young and attractive. As quickly as the thought had come, he brushed it away.

"I'm sorry too, Ramon," she said, laying a hand on his arm. "I should have realized how personal this is to you . . . with . . . what happened to Rosa. And truly, I hadn't planned to go out alone, but . . ." She withdrew her hand and tried to explain. "Itzel became ill; I believe she has a fever. I offered to let her lie down in my cottage until her grandmother came, but she refused. I made the same offer to the grandmother when she arrived, and even offered to have Carolyn take a look at her, but she refused. She seemed determined to walk Itzel home, despite the fact that the poor girl could barely stand up. That's when I knew I had to go along and help them."

Ramon raised his eyebrows. "You went to their home?"

Julia nodded. "Not inside, of course. Just to the doorway. The grandmother thanked me and went inside."

"Did you see anyone else? A father or mother? Sisters or brothers?"

She shook her head. "No. I got the impression it's just the two of them."

Ramon was impressed, but also concerned. "Were there others around? Watching you when you arrived?"

She nodded again. "Yes. Mostly from their doorways. No one spoke or acknowledged my presence in any way. Just stared—glared, actually."

"Exactly what I would expect. You are not welcome there, you know. Neither am I."

"I sensed that. But . . ." She took a half step toward him. "Padre, if we're not welcome there, why does the old woman bring Itzel here to school each day?"

Ramon shrugged. "That is a question I have asked myself many times. I have no answer. Sometimes we have to be grateful, even if we don't understand. This is one of those cases."

The air hung silent between them for a moment, and then Julia turned back toward her home. "I must go. I have papers to correct and lessons to prepare. Have a nice evening."

"And you as well, señora." He watched her disappear inside before returning to his own modest dwelling.

$$\star \; \star \; \star$$

IT WAS **T**HURSDAY BEFORE **I**TZEL returned to school. Not a word was spoken regarding her illness, though Julia thought she appeared to be back to her usual healthy self. The child simply returned to sitting quietly in the classroom, doing her assignments without complaint or comment, and then waiting on the bench after school until her grandmother came to pick her up.

The old woman also said nothing, not even acknowledging Julia with a nod, but Julia felt that somehow they had made a fraction of an inch of progress, though she'd be hard-pressed to explain why she felt that way.

More than once over the next week, she thought about returning to the old woman's home and asking permission to come inside and visit. But each time she considered it, she quickly talked herself out of it. Not only had she been continually warned not to leave the compound alone, but she also knew she would not be welcome in the little breeze-block community. For now she would have to be content with trying to break through the little girl's protective shell as they sat together on the bench each afternoon. Though to date they'd not had an actual conversation, at least Julia sensed the child no longer resented her presence. It was something.

In the meantime, Julia had once again attended the Wednesday evening service at the little chapel. The songs were beginning to sound somewhat familiar to her, and she was becoming more and more interested in and impressed with the simple messages Padre Ramon presented to his little flock.

And now another Sunday had rolled around. Julia surprised herself when she awoke with a sense of anticipation. She realized she was now going to the church services willingly, rather than out of obligation. It was something she hadn't experienced since she was a child attending Sunday School.

She picked out a simple cotton dress, pink with embroidered flowers, and headed for the door. The minute she stepped outside and into the cold gray morning fog, she quickly turned back to grab her favorite white shawl. Tossing it around her shoulders, she went on her way.

★ CHAPTER 12 ★

JULIA HAD BECOME ACCUSTOMED to hearing the gentle strains of Padre Ramon's guitar as she entered the quaint little house of worship. But she was caught off-guard when he glanced up and met her gaze with his as she made her way to a seat near Frank and Carolyn Barnes. Did she imagine it, or had his eyes lit up as he smiled at her in welcome?

Her cheeks warmed at the thought as she returned his smile and then lowered her eyes, as if concentrating on the floor as she settled into a chair. What had gotten into her? She hadn't acted like this since she was a college girl, enamored of the tall, handsome Tom Bennington, who had so totally won her heart as well as her hand in marriage. Ramon was nothing like Tom—nothing at all. And she was no longer a college girl. She was a middle-aged widow with grown children, for pity's sake, and she reminded herself to behave accordingly.

Julia had taken a seat beside the center aisle, on the end of a row of six chairs. Carolyn sat immediately to her left, with Frank just beyond that. Carolyn offered her a smile and a pat on her hand when Julia looked over at her.

"So glad you're here," Carolyn whispered. "You look lovely in pink. But then, you always look lovely." She turned to her husband. "Doesn't she, Frank?"

Frank's heavy eyebrows rose. He'd been reading from the Bible that lay open on his lap. "Excuse me? Did you say something?"

Carolyn leaned closer to him. "I said that Julia always looks lovely, but especially so today in her pink dress. Don't you agree?"

Frank still appeared confused, or possibly embarrassed, but he nodded quickly. "Sure. Of course she does." After a brief smile in Julia's direction, he returned to his reading.

The soft guitar music shifted to singing, and the congregation rose and joined their voices with the pastor's. Julia did the same, but she was careful to avoid looking straight at Ramon. The poor man was simply trying to be kind, which was his nature; he wasn't in any way interested in Julia as a woman. It was obvious he'd been very much in love with his wife and still grieved her death. Julia resolved to keep that in mind.

When the singing concluded and the worshippers had once again taken their seats and the pastor asked them to turn in their Bibles to the first chapter of Second Timothy, her cheeks warmed again. She had vowed on Wednesday night to start bringing her Bible to the services so she could follow along with everyone else, but she'd forgotten all about it until now. It simply wasn't something she was used to doing, though her parents wouldn't dream of going to church without theirs.

Self-consciously she cut her eyes to the left and followed along in Carolyn's Bible, glad the older woman used one with large print. At some point Carolyn must have realized what Julia was doing and slid the Bible slightly to the right to make it easier for Julia to read.

After the pastor had finished reading the entire first chapter, he looked out over his flock, his face soft with compassion as he spoke to them in Spanish. "That passage of Scripture is a strong call to loyalty and courage, one that applied not only to the young man Timothy but to all believers throughout the ages. But I will confess to you that when I truly stop and think about that, I become uncomfortable. I immediately have to ask myself how loyal and courageous I really am when it comes to taking a stand for my faith."

Julia lifted her eyebrows in surprise. Somehow she had never imagined the gentle pastor as being anything but strong in his faith. Hadn't he continued his ministry among the very people who may very well have been involved in his wife's death? True, he had moved his family inside the walls of the compound, but that was for the safety of his children. It had been the right thing to do, the wise thing. And though the man had never shown her anything but a humble spirit, she had never doubted that his faith was solid. In fact, more than once since coming to La Paz she had found herself wishing her own faith was half as strong.

"The key," Padre Ramon said, "is focusing on verse 7, which tells us that 'God has not given us a spirit of fear, but of power and of love and of a sound mind.' What does that mean?"

He paused, as if waiting for someone to respond. Of course, no one did, and Julia waited, curious to hear what the pastor would say.

"In order to answer that question," he continued, "we have to remember that the Apostle Paul was talking to his young protégé, Timothy, about using his God-given gifts in a powerful and effective way. He wasn't saying that we should never feel fear because there are times when fear can warn us away from danger or stop us from doing something foolish. The type of fear Paul is talking about here is the kind that keeps us from stepping out in faith and obeying God's call on our life. That's what he wanted Timothy to understand. The young man was intimidated by his own youth and inexperience, but Paul was telling him that such fear did not come from God. If God had gifted and called him to do something—which He most certainly had—then Timothy didn't have to depend on himself to accomplish it. All he had to do was say yes to God and take that first step; God would give him power and strength he needed to do the rest."

The words echoed in Julia's ears. No doubt she'd heard these very verses many times throughout her growing-up years in Sunday School and church, but never had they impacted her the way they did at this moment. The rest of Ramon's words faded into the distance as she pondered the ones he had already spoken.

Was it possible God had called her here, to this very place at this exact time in history? The thought seemed ludicrous. She believed in God, yes, and had heard throughout her lifetime that she needed a personal relationship with Him, but beyond receiving Jesus as her Savior when she was a little girl, she'd never pursued it any further. She'd often considered that she probably needed to make her faith more personal, but how was she to do that? And yet, wouldn't it have to be so in order to know for certain that God had called you to something and would give you the strength to fulfill His calling if you simply agreed to do it? Before you could say yes to His call, wouldn't you first have to hear and recognize His voice?

She was still wrestling with those questions when the pastor finished his sermon and invited the congregation to stand for the closing hymn and benediction.

★ ★ ★

OCTOBER WAS NEARLY OVER, but the weather in Temecula still said summer. It was Marie's favorite time of year. As she steered her car toward Old Town, where she would meet Ginny for lunch, it was the last Wednesday of the month and she couldn't help but think of the many autumns she'd enjoyed with Julia when she was young.

She loved all the fall holidays—dressing up and decorating for them, baking and cooking special foods. But it really all started when it was time to go back to school. How she looked forward to that each year! While other children moaned and groaned about saying good-bye to summer vacation, Julia was up bright and early, dressed and ready to go well before the bus arrived. Even when we moved from Imperial Beach to Temecula, she adjusted and excelled in her studies. It's no surprise she ended up being such a fine teacher.

Her heart twitched at the reminder of where Julia was now. Marie braked at a red light just before the entrance to Old Town and tried to picture the compound where her daughter now lived and worked. Julia had managed to text a couple of pictures, but it wasn't the same as being there, and part of her wished she could be.

Why? she asked herself, moving ahead when the light turned green. *Do I really think I could protect her somehow?* She sighed. *Only You can do that, Lord. I know that, but . . . do I ever stop being a mom?*

She nearly laughed aloud at the ludicrous question. Of course she would never stop being a mom, but at some point didn't she have to relinquish her grown daughter—a middle-aged daughter at that—into her heavenly Father's hands?

That's the real problem, Lord. If only she would truly give her heart and life to You, what a difference that would make! How long must I pray for that to happen, Father? How long?

Another ludicrous question, she realized. "For as long as it takes," she said aloud, spotting the restaurant up ahead. "As long as I have breath in my body."

She pulled into the nearly full parking lot, found an empty space not far from Ginny's car, and resolved to put her concerns for Julia on the back burner for the next hour or two. Ginny was a wonderful friend, and they hadn't done something special like this in a very long time. They were overdue.

★ ★ ★

AFTER LESS THAN A TEN-MINUTE WAIT, Marie and Ginny were seated, ice waters in front of them and menus in hand.

"What are you hungry for?" Marie asked, browsing the lunch specials.

"Everything." Ginny giggled. "But don't let me order that. I'm supposed to be watching my weight." She laughed again. "Seems lately, all I do is watch it climb."

Marie looked up from her menu and across the table at her friend. "I understand only too well." She smiled. "I remember the good old days, when I could eat anything I wanted and work it off by nighttime."

Ginny nodded, her brown eyes dancing. "Oh yeah, those were the days for sure! But no more." She shook her head. "I used to laugh at people who said all they had to do was look at food and they gained weight. Now I'm beginning to understand."

She sighed. "Still, even though I know I should be good, I really can't get excited about a side salad with lemon juice for dressing."

"Neither can I." Marie looked back at her menu. "In fact, I'm leaning toward the Reuben sandwich. Maybe it wouldn't be so bad if I substitute a salad for the fries."

"We'll make that a double order, and we're set," Ginny said, folding her menu and setting it on the edge of the table. They both laughed as Marie placed her own menu on top of Ginny's.

"So," Ginny said, "now that we've settled the food issue, how's everything else going? Have you heard from Julia?"

"Not since I last talked to you," Marie admitted. "It's tough getting only sporadic emails, but she sends a letter faithfully each week. From what she says, it sounds as if she's settled in well and enjoys what she's doing."

"Good for her. I'm glad she decided to take advantage of this opportunity, aren't you?"

Before Marie could answer, the waitress arrived at their table, pen and tablet in hand. By the time they finished ordering, Marie dared to hope Ginny would forget her unanswered question and move on to something else. It didn't happen.

"We were talking about Julia," Ginny said before the waitress had gotten more than a half dozen steps away from their table. "You're pleased that she's enjoying her experience, right?"

Marie hedged, not wanting to lie but not wanting to admit that she wished her only child were safe and sound in her own home. "She does seem to be enjoying it, and I'm glad for that."

Ginny raised her penciled-in eyebrows. "But . . .?"

Marie sighed. She couldn't get much past this woman. "But . . . I still worry. To be honest, I wish she hadn't gone. And I blame myself for that. She wouldn't even have known about it if I hadn't opened my big mouth."

Ginny smiled and reached across the table to pat Marie's hand. "Stop blaming yourself. Who knows? Maybe God used you to prompt Julia into going on this trip. If it's His purpose for her to be there, then you can thank yourself for your part in it all."

"I suppose." Marie wished she could be more enthusiastic, but Ginny would have seen through it anyway. "She's been gone a couple of months now, and so far everything seems to be going well. Maybe I'm worried about nothing, but I won't rest until she comes home in June."

Ginny's eyebrows lifted again. "She doesn't come back until then? I hadn't realized it was such a long commitment."

Marie nodded and took a sip of her water. "A school year. Then she'll begin preparing for the new school year here when she gets back."

Ginny played with the straw in her own water glass, twirling it slowly but never taking a drink. "I still think it's good for her. She'll come home with memories she'll treasure for the rest of her life—and who knows what else? Trips like this can change someone's life forever."

Marie frowned. "True. I just hope it's for the better."

Their waitress arrived with their salads then, and Marie reached for her fork with relief. Maybe now they could finally stop talking about Julia. She bowed her head to offer silent thanks for her food, but Ginny was one step ahead of her.

"Thank You, Lord, for this food You've provided for us, and for the time You've given us to spend together. May we honor You in all we say and do this day. And, Father, please reassure Marie's heart that You have Your protective hand on Julia. Amen."

"Amen," Marie whispered, blinking back a sudden onslaught of tears as she realized how grateful she was to have such a dear and faithful friend as Ginny—and such a powerful and faithful God who loved her daughter even more than she did.

★ CHAPTER 13 ★

HERNANDO WAS FRUSTRATED—furious, really. He'd accomplished exactly what he'd set out do—kidnap tourists, obtain a ransom for them, and then release them without serious injury, nearly guaranteeing that no legal action or consequences would follow. But apparently that wasn't enough to exonerate him for his one past failure. Now he had been instructed to do it again—and soon.

He shook his head as he lay on the lumpy bed in the room he shared with one of his compadres. Raul snored like an angry bull, so much so that Hernando had escaped to the old building behind the house to try and catch some sleep on the old mattress on the floor. Tonight he had too much on his mind anyway, so there seemed to be no point in tossing and turning beside his snoring friend.

How many times will I have to do this before I earn my way back in? I'm sick of this place. I want to go back to Guadalajara where I belong.

The image of the thriving metropolis with its pulsating nightlife plagued his thoughts, causing him to hate his seclusion in this old Mayan stronghold in Chiapas State more by the day. Besides, he was getting sick of San Cristobal. San Juan Chamula was smaller, but at least it was a change of pace. He decided to head over there in the next few days and check it out. Tourists visited there too, so why not go for a little variety? But this time he was determined to find a woman who still had some life in her. Why not take advantage while waiting for the ransom delivery?

With that thought dancing through his mind and a smile playing on his lips, he closed his eyes and soon fell asleep.

★ ★ ★

ITZEL'S THICK, STRAIGHT HAIR SHONE almost blue-black in the afternoon sunshine. Julia was pleased to see how she entered into this preplanned "workday." Julia had decided to take the students outside to enjoy the lovely autumn weather in an experiment that she believed would show them more about cooperation and working together than anything she could try to teach them in the classroom.

The last few remaining ears of corn needed to be harvested and the weeds hoed between the rows of pumpkins and squash. Julia planned to use their shared working experience to teach them about the upcoming American holiday of Thanksgiving.

She smiled at the thought as she wielded her own hoe, enjoying the feel of the warm noonday sun on her shoulders. The thought of missing out on their annual family Thanksgiving gathering tugged at her heart, but she knew her parents would put on a great spread for Tyler and Brittney, so she needn't worry that they would be neglected. Besides, the last two Thanksgivings had been tough on her, being in such a familiar setting and sharing so many long-held family traditions and memories yet being unable to block out the glaring absence of her husband, who for years had been the official turkey carver. It was better this way, preparing to celebrate a Thanksgiving with her students, though she doubted it would include a turkey.

Should she invite Padre Ramon? Her heart skipped a beat at the thought, though she did her best to convince herself she had no motive other than including the man who had occasionally helped the Barneses to teach these very students before she arrived, a man the children already loved and respected. Surely it would be the right thing to do under the circumstances.

"Buenos dias, Itzel."

The gentle, masculine voice interrupted Julia's thoughts, and she looked up to find Padre Ramon standing beside Itzel. The girl with the shining hair looked up at him and offered a rare smile. "Buenos dias," she answered, her voice soft.

The padre continued in Spanish. "You are working very hard, I see. Are you enjoying yourself?"

Itzel nodded, her hair shimmering in the sunlight. "Sí, Padre."

He laid a hand on her shoulder. "You are not only a good student but a good worker, as well."

The child's face lit up at the compliment, her gaze remaining on the pastor as he moved through the garden, stopping to call each student by name and to compliment them in some way. Julia's heart squeezed. How could she not admire such a man?

And then he looked up, smiled, and headed in her direction. Julia thought she could hear her heart beating in her ears. She restrained herself from shaking her head in a futile attempt to dislodge the sound.

"Señora Bennington." Ramon stopped a couple feet from her, still smiling.

Julia marveled at the whiteness of his teeth against his olive complexion. She swallowed and did her best to keep her voice steady. "Padre Ramon. How nice of you to come out and visit us."

"I have been watching you . . ." He paused, and she thought she saw his Adam's apple bob up and down before he continued. "All of you, out here working in the garden. I am pleased to see this. It is part of a lesson plan, sí?"

She nodded, suddenly aware of the hoe in her hands and the fact that she was leaning on it. She straightened her shoulders and smiled. "Sí. Yes. I'm preparing to teach them about the American holiday of Thanksgiving." She remembered her recent quandary about inviting the padre to join them. Her eyes still locked into his, she said, "We're going to have a Thanksgiving dinner in the classroom next week—no turkey, of course, but corn and squash and potatoes from the garden. Would you . . . would you like to join us?"

His smile spread, lighting up his eyes. "I would like that very much. But you must let me bring something."

Bring something? Did he understand that this wasn't a formal dinner, just a teaching tool to help the students learn about the purpose of Thanksgiving and how it came to be a holiday?

Before she could voice her questions, he said, "I understand it will only be a small meal, but I want the students to see that we each contribute something to share with the others. That's your purpose in having them work together on the food they will eat at this Thanksgiving meal, am I right?"

He was right indeed. And she was more than pleased to know he would be there to celebrate with them. She nodded. "Yes. Absolutely. We will be happy to have you join us, Padre."

After a brief moment, he nodded once and turned. She watched him until he was back inside the little church where he would no doubt be working on his next sermon.

★ ★ ★

TYLER AND BRITTNEY HAD LONG SINCE gotten past their spat in the library, chalking it up to one of many they'd had over the years. They loved one another and instinctively knew they would never let anything come between them.

For that reason Tyler made a point of crisscrossing the campus on Sunday afternoon, hitting all of Brittney's favorite haunts until he found her under a tree behind her dorm. It was a great spot to catch the afternoon rays, and Tyler couldn't help but notice how her unruly hair burned a reddish hue that blended in with the many fallen leaves that dotted the area.

"Hey," he said in greeting, walking up and plopping down beside her. The grass felt cool but not wet, so he settled in comfortably next to her, not concerned that he might stain his jeans.

"Hey, yourself." She flipped off her ereader and set it aside. "What's up?"

He shrugged. "Just thinking that it's almost Thanksgiving. You still want to go home, right? Even though Mom won't be there?"

She frowned. "Of course I do. Where else would I go on Thanksgiving? We'll eat at Grandma and Grandpa's like we always do."

"Yeah, I guess." Tyler tried to ignore the words he wanted to say about their mom being gone, as he knew they would only serve to resurrect their previous disagreements on the subject.

"What does that mean?"

He should have known she'd call him on it, but he determined not to take the bait. "Nothing." He shrugged again. "Just thought we should talk about what time we want to leave. We should probably call Grandma too and make sure dinner's still at the usual time."

Brittney grinned. "You know Grandma won't care what time we come, so long as we get there—and the sooner the better. Cooking the Thanksgiving meal is her *thing*, as Grandpa calls it."

Tyler chuckled. "Yeah, that's true. So when's your last class get out on Wednesday?"

"I should be done and ready to go no later than 3:00."

"Perfect. I'll meet you in the parking lot in front of my dorm then."

He stood to his feet, brushed off the seat of his pants, and walked away.

★ CHAPTER 14 ★

JULIA AND CAROLYN HAD SPENT much of Monday afternoon at the large outdoor market in San Juan Chamula, carefully choosing spices and condiments and even some cocoa to complement the fruits and vegetables they already cultivated in their garden at the compound. Julia wanted their Thanksgiving meal to be not only meaningful to the children but delicious as well. It was the first time she'd be away from her family for the holiday, and the first time her meal would not include a large roasted turkey.

Now, as the children gathered excitedly this Tuesday afternoon around the long makeshift table and benches that Padre Ramon and Frank Barnes had set up earlier in the day, Julia smiled. The tears that stung her eyes were bittersweet, as she pictured her children and parents gathering together on Thursday for their traditional meal without her. Yet she was also pleased at her students' willingness to learn of an American holiday.

Carolyn and Frank Barnes had gone into town on previously scheduled errands, so that left Julia and Ramon to oversee the children. *Not a problem,* Julia mused. *These kids are so well behaved. If my high schoolers back home were half this disciplined, teaching would be a snap.*

Three of the girls, including Marina, were busy setting out plates of corn, potatoes, black beans, and baked squash, all fresh from the garden the children had helped to cultivate. They had all pitched in to help with the cooking in Julia's small kitchen, and then setting the table. None of them knew that Julia had spent the last evening baking them a chocolate cake for dessert, but she imagined they would be pleased when she brought it out later.

Warm sunlight shone on their backs, with only a slight breeze to keep them comfortable. It seemed even the birds and monkeys chimed in to help them celebrate this special occasion.

When all the children were seated, even those who had been carrying the food from the kitchen, Julia realized there were only two seats left, side by side. Her cheeks warmed as she took one of them, aware that the other was reserved for Padre Ramon, who was just now making his way toward them. The children returned his greeting as he sat down in the only empty chair, but not before catching Julia's eyes and offering a hesitant smile.

Julia hoped her own smile looked more natural than it felt, as they all folded their hands and bowed their heads, waiting for the padre to offer a prayer of thanks. Julia scarcely heard his words, as she concentrated on trying to ignore the man's closeness. This particular scenario had never occurred to her when she invited him to join them for their meal, but it was only right that he should be here. She realized then that if he hadn't come, it would have been up to her to offer the blessing. Though she'd sat through enough Thanksgiving prayers in her lifetime to believe she could do so, she was relieved the task hadn't fallen to her.

Why am I so uncomfortable about anything related to faith? I was raised in it, after all. And I'm getting used to the weekly services here at La Paz. But as soon as it becomes personal, I find myself withdrawing. She frowned. *Why is that? It's not that I don't believe in God, and yet . . .*

Padre Ramon ended his prayer with a hearty amen, echoed by the children, and it was time to eat. Julia chased the thoughts from her mind and began to pass the heaping bowls of food around the table. This might be the most unusual Thanksgiving dinner she'd ever experienced, but she was determined it would also be a joyous one.

★ ★ ★

MARIE HAD BEEN UP SINCE BEFORE DAYLIGHT, stuffing the twenty-pound turkey and getting it ready to pop into the oven, preparing snacks, and fussing with last-minute decorations and place settings at the table. Tyler and Brittney had arrived the night before and were both upstairs sleeping in.

"You're going to wear yourself out before dinner," John warned as he entered the kitchen midmorning. "Take it easy, sweetheart. It's just our grandkids here for dinner, not the queen of England."

Marie stopped in the middle of rearranging the napkins one more time. She looked up at him and raised her eyebrows. "I'd rather cook for my family than the queen of England any day. I want them to know how special they are and how glad we are that they're with us, especially now that . . ."

Her voice trailed off as hot tears sprang into her eyes. She saw her husband's face go soft, and she knew he too was thinking how different Thanksgiving would be this year without their daughter at the table. She blinked the tears away and returned to her task, her head bowed. "It's bad enough our grandchildren have lost their father, but now their mother has taken off on some wild goose chase, teaching children in the middle of God-knows-where, so it's up to us to pick up the slack."

John came to stand behind her and slipped his arms around her ample waist. "I miss her too, and I know it's going to be like having dinner with the proverbial elephant in the room without her, but what else can we do? Of course we have to make it as easy on the kids as we can, but no amount of fussing or primping is going to erase what they're feeling today."

The tears Marie had been holding back spilled over then, and she turned and buried her face in her husband's chest, glad for the strength he offered as he held her close. If only her daughter were somewhere more civilized and safe, maybe her temporary absence would be easier to accept.

But she wasn't, and until this awful time was over and Julia came home where she belonged, Marie doubted she would ever be at peace with the situation. She'd prayed and prayed, and tried to turn it over to God countless times, but always her fears came back to haunt her. There were times she was certain she simply couldn't bear it for another day, but she really had no choice, and so she pressed on.

★ ★ ★

BRITTNEY AWOKE AHEAD OF **T**YLER and managed to get showered and dressed before he started banging on the guest bathroom door.

"You going to stay in there forever?" he hollered.

She smiled, taking just an extra minute for a final few tweaks to her makeup. This reminded her of their growing-up years, when they shared a bathroom and Tyler never stopped complaining that she took more than her share of time in there.

"I might," she answered, grinning at herself in the mirror. Her red-gold locks were still wet and clipped on top of her head. Should she make him wait longer while she styled them? She shook her head. No sense torturing the poor guy.

She opened the door, leaving the light on. "It's all yours, bro."

He brushed past her, closed the door, and flipped the lock, seemingly all in one motion. Chuckling, she headed for the stairs, her mouth already salivating at the pumpkin and spice smells making their way up toward her. It wouldn't be long until the delectable aroma of roasting turkey would join in, making the wait nearly unbearable.

Grandma always has snacks to tide us over, and she'll no doubt want to stop what she's doing and fix us breakfast, but I'm going to stick with coffee and save my appetite for dinner.

She smiled at the thought that she made that resolution every year, but the minute she spotted all the goodies her grandmother had set out for everyone to munch on, her resolve when down the drain.

Just give up and dive in. You know you're going to anyway. Brittney could hear her mother's voice, urging her on, and the memory sent a jagged pain slicing through her heart.

Mom's not here. First Dad, and now Mom. Aren't families supposed to grow through the years? Ours is just getting smaller.

Before the sadness that still washed over her since her father's death could once again grab hold of her and ruin her day, she took a deep breath, pasted a smile on her face, and headed for the kitchen to see what she could do to help.

★ CHAPTER 15 ★

ITZEL THOUGHT THE HOLIDAY called Thanksgiving was a very good one indeed, though she said nothing about it to her abuela. The young girl of Mayan ancestry knew her grandmother took a great chance in defying the old ways and allowing her granddaughter to attend school at the compound. None of her friends were so blessed, and Itzel was indeed happy for the opportunity.

Still, she knew her place and knew not to cross certain lines with her abuela. The old woman had cared for her since her parents died, so long ago the girl could not remember them. The few times she had dared to ask her abuela how her parents had died, the woman had silenced her with a look. As much as Itzel loved her abuela, she also feared her, though the woman had never harmed her in any way.

"It is dangerous to cross the old ways," she had once whispered to her granddaughter, sending shivers down the girl's spine. "We must be very careful."

And yet, when Señor and Señora Barnes had come to their neighborhood that one time and knocked on doors to invite the children to come to school, Abuela had dared to accept the invitation, being careful to walk Itzel to and from the compound, cautioning her never to do so on her own.

She sat outside now, in the dirt yard in front of the one-room, thatched-roof home she shared with her grandmother. Chickens scratched around her, even as the girl made her own marks in the dirt, using a stick to practice the letters she was learning at school. There was no school today, as Señora Bennington had explained that

Thanksgiving was a holiday in the place faraway where she and the Barneses were from. Itzel missed being at school, but practicing her letters in the dirt, with the warm noonday sunshine overhead, was a pleasant way to pass the day.

"Itzel, come here."

Her abuela's voice interrupted her thoughts. She laid down her stick, stood up and brushed the dirt from her hands, and hurried inside.

"Take a shawl," Abuela instructed, already wrapped in her own and carrying the colorful shopping bag she used when they went to the outdoor food market to barter or trade. "I need some *chipilín* to spice up our dinner, so we will take potatoes and corn from the garden to trade."

The girl grabbed her worn blue shawl and threw it over her shoulders as she turned and skipped out the door ahead of her abuela. A trip to the market was always an interesting adventure. Perhaps her abuela would even find a way to get her a piece of candied fruit, though it wouldn't be nearly as good as the chocolate cake she'd had the day before.

★ ★ ★

HERNANDO WAS GROWING TIRED of the constant pressure to deliver more ransom money. Hadn't he explained that it would be easier if they'd left him in Guadalajara or at least sent him to some other good-sized city where the tourists were more plentiful? Of course he had, but his words had fallen on deaf ears. The orders to prove himself once again were now couched in threats, and he knew he was running out of time.

The first couple had been easy, but he hadn't come across anyone quite so vulnerable since then. If they would be more patient, no doubt he would locate his next victims and be able to obtain more money. But he couldn't snatch just anyone, could he? He needed to be reasonably certain the person had relatives with money who cared enough to pay it.

Annoyed with his compadres, he decided to take a little trip into San Juan Chamula. He'd driven through it a time or two, but he'd never had time to hang around the tourist areas and check out the possibilities. This sunny Thursday afternoon seemed exactly the right time to do that.

He hopped into the beat-up white Chevy Blazer that had become his only ride since his foolish indiscretion had cost him nearly everything but his life—and even that could be snatched away at any time. He drove the short distance from San Cristobal to Chamula in well under thirty minutes, despite being delayed behind an overpacked bus full of an almost equal number of animals and people. *But no one worth any money,* he thought, as he watched the weary riders disembark in front of the San Juan Chamula bus station.

Driving a bit farther he found himself close enough to the outdoor market to park his Blazer and go the rest of the way on foot.

Stupid people stink worse than the animals, he thought, as he pushed his way through the crowds. Women bartered for food, while children clung to their long skirts. Buying a warm tamale, which he was told contained armadillo meat but was convinced was really from a dog, he munched on it as he made his way up one aisle and down the next, only to return to his vehicle empty-handed.

Disgusted, he cursed and threw the empty banana leaf from his tamale on the ground. He glared at a little girl who stared at him, wide-eyed, then climbed into his car and took off, kicking up dust on all who stood in his wake.

★ ★ ★

ITZEL WAS PLEASED that her abuela had been able to trade her vegetables for the spices she needed as well as a slice of candied mango. The girl sucked on it, wanting it to last as long as possible as they prepared to leave the market and head home.

The sun was starting to ease its way down now, and the air grew cool. Itzel managed to cling to the corners of her shawl as she savored her tasty treat. She and her abuela hadn't gone far when Itzel heard a man utter a word she didn't understand, but she could tell from the anger in his voice that it was not a nice word. Still clutching her shawl and her mango slice, she looked up in time to see a mean-looking man throw a tamale wrapper on the ground. Her eyes went wide when he caught her looking at him just before he climbed into his vehicle, and she moved closer to her abuela, averting her gaze.

She heard the vehicle's door slam and the engine roar to life before the man drove down the dirt road, spraying dust into her eyes and onto her mango. Itzel looked up from her damaged treat at the white vehicle and watched it disappear around a corner. She wasn't sure if the tears she felt stinging her eyes were from the dust she'd gotten in them or because the man had ruined her mango.

"It is all right, little one." Her abuela's voice was hushed as she patted Itzel's shoulder. "We will wash your fruit in the water bucket when we get home."

Itzel lifted her head, surprised at her abuela's kind words. The woman spoke very little, and her rare assurance warmed the young girl's heart. She smiled up at her, but Abuela didn't see. Her eyes were straight ahead as they walked, looking in the direction where the mean man in the white vehicle had disappeared. Suddenly the little girl wanted nothing more than to get back to the safety of their home and hide away there with their chickens and their garden.

★ CHAPTER 16 ★

JULIA HAD HOPED to be able to connect with her parents and children on Thanksgiving Day via the Internet, but it hadn't worked out. Instead she'd spent the evening writing long letters to each of them after having a small but enjoyable Thanksgiving meal with the Barneses and Padre Ramon. But as nice as the meal and fellowship had been, it didn't compare to her warm memories of the early Thanksgiving celebration she'd shared with Ramon and the children.

She smiled at the memory, comparing it to the many family-filled Thanksgivings of her past. There was no comparison, of course, and though her heart squeezed at missing out on the day with her parents and children—not to mention the fact that she would never again enjoy such a time with her late husband—she knew she wouldn't give up the once-in-a-lifetime experience she'd had with her students.

And Ramon, she thought, then quickly banished the images of his warm laughter and his pleasant voice as he led the children in singing after their meal. It had indeed been a delightful day, and it was representative of her entire experience so far here at La Paz. How could she have doubted for a moment the rightness of taking advantage of this rare opportunity? She would go home a better person for it and was certain her family would recognize that, even if they didn't understand it now.

Setting her completed letters aside, she made a mental note to take advantage of the fact that she'd opted to give the children the entire weekend off. They wouldn't be back until Monday, so that meant she was free on Friday. As soon as the usual morning fog burned off, she would venture out for a brief walk to town, where she would mail her letters and browse the outdoor market a bit before coming back. She'd been there several times now, though never alone, except for the time she'd walked with Itzel and her *abuela,* and she'd never seen any reason for concern. It was perfectly safe, and so long as she didn't alarm the Barneses or Ramon by telling them of her plans, she'd be back before they even realized she was gone.

She stood and stretched, then changed into her pajamas and slipped under the covers. The novel she was reading beckoned to her from the nightstand beside her bed, so she picked it up and began to read. She knew it wouldn't be long before her eyes grew heavy and she turned out the light, but for now it was an enjoyable pastime in a place that sported no televisions, only one radio, and very sporadic Internet service. It was a pace of life that she was beginning to think suited her well.

★ ★ ★

HERNANDO HADN'T SLEPT MUCH. In addition to his snoring roommate, his mind raced with the pressures he felt to deliver more ransom money. Obviously he couldn't do that until he kidnapped someone, and that someone had to have the strong possibility of relatives willing and able to pay the ransom.

If he just had more time, he could wait for the perfect tourist to show up, as had happened last time. But he didn't have time; he was going to have to make a move soon. His trip to San Juan Chamula on Thursday hadn't produced any promising leads—except one. When he'd returned and his compadres had asked where he'd been, he told them of the reason for his foray into Chamula. That's when Raul had mentioned seeing a couple of *gringas* in town the last time he was there. He'd asked around about them and learned they were from the La

Paz Compound. He also found out they were *Americanas,* meaning the possibility of their families having money was strong.

Hernando had nearly knocked the idiot in the head for not telling him about this sooner but now, after thinking about it all night, he had decided to drive back into Chamula to see if he could learn more about these women. Perhaps one or both of them could prove to be the answer to his problem.

★ ★ ★

THE MORNING FOG had been slower than usual to burn off, but Julia had wrapped her favorite white shawl around her shoulders and headed out anyway. She wanted to get an early start before the Barneses or Padre Ramon were out and about and more apt to see her leave. If all went well, she'd be back before they missed her. She didn't want anyone to worry, but she was looking forward to a pleasant outing on her own.

She went first to the post office to make sure her letters would go out that day. After that she turned her attention to some browsing at the outdoor marketplace.

The aroma of freshly baked tamales snagged her attention, and she spotted a street vendor selling them near the entrance to the marketplace. Her stomach growled with anticipation, as she realized she hadn't yet had any breakfast. What better than one of the local steamed black bean-and-masa treats? She knew many of the tamales also contained such ingredients as iguana or fish, but she opted to stick with what she considered safer and more familiar ingredients.

She stopped in front of the vendor's cart and asked in Spanish for one tamale, beans only. The old man with the nearly black eyes frowned suspiciously. Wordlessly he handed her a banana-leaf tamale, still warm from the steamer. She paid him, smiling as she spoke her thanks. Still he did not respond, and so she took her breakfast and moved on, sensing that he watched her as she walked away.

Spotting an empty bench she sat down on one end of it and unwrapped her tamale. The tantalizing smell grew stronger, and her mouth watered. She was about to bite into it when the image of Padre Ramon offering thanks at the table where the children were assembled for their group meal stopped her. Praying before she ate was a habit she'd grown up with but hadn't continued to practice as an adult. Today, as the morning sun began to burn through the fog in this delightful little Mayan village, she found herself wanting to do so.

She bowed her head and closed her eyes. *Thank You, God, for this food,* she prayed silently, *and for this beautiful morning.* She hesitated yet again, and then continued. *I know I haven't talked to You much lately, but I truly do appreciate the chance to come here. Amen.*

Opening her eyes, she allowed herself to bite into the warm tamale. The slightly sweet spices complemented the rich black beans and soft masa, and she wondered if she'd ever had such a delicious breakfast anywhere before.

The sun warmed her shoulders now as she ate, and she sat where she was for a few minutes, watching the foot traffic increase around her as more and more people arrived to do their daily shopping at the marketplace. At last she decided it was time to join them and make her own purchases so she could get back to the compound before anyone got worried and came looking for her.

She stood, placed her now empty banana leaf in her bright-red floral print shopping bag until she could find an appropriate place to dispose of it, and then began her stroll down the first aisle, checking out the many offerings of fruit and vegetables, spices and pastries, and even homemade jewelry and clothing.

Mom and Brittney would love this place. I know it's a little too soon now, but I'm definitely going to get them souvenirs from here before I go back to the States.

Thirty minutes and a handful of items later, Julia decided it was well past time to head back. With the sun now at its fullest, she folded her shawl, placed it into her shopping bag with her other items, and turned toward the compound.

★ CHAPTER 17 ★

By the time Hernando rolled into San Juan Chamula, it was midmorning and the sun had burned through the fog, leaving a warm, pleasant day as the town's residents mixed with tourists at the marketplace. But Hernando didn't care about the comfortable temperatures or pleasant surroundings; he had a purpose and he was determined to fulfill it.

He parked his old Blazer near the same place he'd left it the day before, but this time he bypassed the tamale vendor and headed straight for the stalls that lined the aisles of the marketplace. He ignored the fruits and vegetables, the fish and iguanas and armadillos, the jewelry and clothing, his eyes searching up and down each row, hoping to spot the American women Raul had told him about. The description wasn't as detailed as Hernando would have liked, but enough that he thought he would recognize them if he saw them— especially the one with the red hair.

A handful of tourists were sprinkled among the locals, and he eyed them closely, wondering if the women were among them or if another tourist would do. But he saw no one that resembled the women Raul had described; the only tourists he spotted were in groups and not nearly accessible or vulnerable enough for his purposes.

Catching the eye of an old man selling vegetables, he decided to take a chance and ask if he'd seen a couple of American women from the La Paz Compound. The man shook his head no. Then Hernando decided to take one more chance. In fluent Spanish and trying to keep his question as casual as possible, he asked, "Do you know where the compound is? It is near here, yes?"

The old man squinted his eyes warily, as if contemplating whether or not to answer. At last he nodded. "Sí," he answered, pointing in a direction away from the marketplace and toward the forest.

Hernando knew that was all he was going to get out of the ancient vegetable vendor, so he muttered a quick "gracias" and turned to head back toward his vehicle. It was then that he spotted her—an attractive middle-aged woman carrying a shopping bag. She looked American, and though there was only one woman and not two, Hernando couldn't help but smile as he saw the sun glint off her short red curls.

It must be her. Raul described her hair just so.

He quickly set his pace to follow her as she seemed to be making her way out of the marketplace. If she headed in the direction of the compound, he'd know for sure it was her.

In moments he was certain he was following the right woman. Not only was she walking in the direction of La Paz, but he could tell from her walk and the way she carried herself that she was a woman of standing, one who no doubt had people who cared for her and would gladly pay money to get her back.

A do-gooder. They come to our country all the time, especially in the big cities. They try to make themselves feel better about their wealth by working in the orphanages or helping to build houses. He snorted. *But then they go back to their own big houses and fancy cars and forget the people here who can never leave.*

Hernando nodded to himself as he climbed into his Blazer and started it up. He would follow close enough not to lose her but not so close that she would notice. *And then we will find out how classy this* gringa *really is. I like older women with experience, and though I wasn't interested in the last one we had, I will make sure to have time alone with this one. She is very beautiful for her age, and she looks like she might enjoy a little company from a handsome younger man like me.* He laughed aloud as he pressed on the gas and proceeded slowly down the road toward the forest, careful not to kick up any dust as he had when he left town the day before. Unlike yesterday, today he would take his time, and he sensed he would be rewarded for his patience—in more ways than one.

★ ★ ★

THE WARM SUN, combined with the heady smells of flowering plants and the occasional bird and monkey calls coming from the surrounding rain forest, made Julia's walk back to the compound delightful. The scarcely traveled dirt road where she walked seemed almost reserved for her, with the exception of a couple of stray dogs that passed her along the way and what sounded like an old truck chugging slowly somewhere behind her. No one seemed to be in a hurry.

She smiled at the slow pace that was becoming more acceptable to her by the day. *I would love to bring Tyler and Brittney down here. I'd have a hard time convincing them to come, but once they did I know they'd learn to enjoy the unique beauty and lifestyle of this almost ancient place.*

Her thoughts turned then to what her grown children might be doing on this day after Thanksgiving. She chuckled. *Sleeping in, no doubt, and then getting up to eat their grandmother's delicious leftovers.* She was pleased to think of her parents and children spending this long weekend together. And then the thought occurred to her that Brittney might have managed to drag her grandmother out for some good old-fashioned "Black Friday" shopping, while Tyler and his grandfather watched football. Yes, that was a very likely scenario.

And next year I'll be right back in the middle of all that— and I'll love it, just as I have in the past. But for now, today, I am so glad to be right here where I am.

She rounded the last bend, and La Paz came into view. She didn't see any frantic search parties scouring around the outside of the compound, so she imagined she'd returned before anyone realized she was gone.

Good. I wouldn't want to worry anyone, but this has been such a nice outing.

She heard the vehicle behind her gaining on her just as she spied some of the most beautiful ti plants she'd seen since arriving in this tropical paradise. Turning toward them she was struck by the rich, varied colors of black and red. The plants seemed to increase in color and size as she followed them into the forest, reminding herself not to go too far. *I'm near the compound now, so it can't hurt to go a little ways further in. These plants are magnificent, and I haven't really taken the time to see them close up like this before.*

The sun grew thinner as it struggled to penetrate the thick foliage of the forest, but Julia scarcely noticed as she moved from one plant to the next, drinking in the beauty of each one. She knew the plants were common here, but for someone who'd seen so few of them in her lifetime, they certainly didn't seem common to her.

I'd better get back, she thought, forcing herself to stop her trek into the forest. *Maybe I'll bring Carolyn with me later and we can explore these some more.*

But before she could act on her decision, an arm wrapped around her waist and she felt a sharp, cold piece of steel against her neck. She yelped in fear and dropped her shopping bag as both her hands flew to her waist in an attempt to dislodge her unknown assailant's arm. The man squeezed her tighter and pressed what she now knew must be a knife harder against her neck. She was certain he had drawn blood.

"Not a sound," a male voice hissed in Spanish. "Come with me and you will not be hurt. If you fight me or scream, I will kill you where you stand."

Julia's thoughts raced, right along with her heart. *How can this be? What's happening? Who is this person? And what does he want from me?*

But even as the many questions swirled through her mind, she knew he told the truth when he said he would kill her if she fought or screamed. She tried to hold as still as possible, though already she was beginning to tremble.

"Very good," said the voice. "Now remain still and quiet while I get you ready."

Ready? Ready for what? Julia felt her eyes grow wide. What was he going to do to her?

It didn't take long to find out. In moments she was blindfolded and gagged, her hands tied behind her back and her feet hobbled together. Then he picked her up and threw her over his shoulder as he carried her from the rain forest to whatever fate awaited her.

★ ★ ★

MARIE WAS RESTLESS. She'd begged off of Brittney's Black Friday shopping trip that morning and stuck around to fix turkey sandwiches for John and Tyler as they plunked down in front of the TV in the family room. She'd never been a football fan, but she'd always enjoyed shopping—though not on such a crazy day as this. Still, she couldn't help but wonder if she'd made a mistake not accompanying her granddaughter to the saturated mall. At least it would have kept her mind off Julia.

Why today, Lord? Why is her absence bothering me so much right now, more even than it did during yesterday's Thanksgiving dinner? What is it, Father?

She heard no answer, no reassuring whisper, or even a sense of peace. Instead her anxiety increased, and she felt compelled to go to her room and pray. She usually spent her prayertime in the old rocker next to her side of the bed, but this time she found herself slipping to her knees. Tears began to drip from her eyes as she leaned her elbows on the bed, folded her hands, and began to beg God to protect Julia from whatever unseen and unknown danger she was now certain her only child faced.

★ CHAPTER 18 ★

RAMON HAD BEEN RESTLESS ALL MORNING. Something didn't feel right, but he couldn't figure it out. He'd spent several hours in prayer and reading the Bible, but he couldn't concentrate. At last he gave up and went outside, thinking to take a walk around the compound.

As they did so often these days, his eyes wandered to the little cottage where the teacher from America lived. *Julia.* He smiled. He thought her name was beautiful—and so was she. In a very different way from his beloved esposa, Rosa, but beautiful nonetheless. And though he tried, time and time again, to keep his mind from straying in her direction, Julia was beginning to occupy more and more of his thoughts every day.

"Good morning, Padre!"

The familiar greeting stopped him between steps, and he turned to find Carolyn Barnes coming up behind him.

"Buenos dias, señora." He smiled, then noticed the slight frown on her otherwise pleasant face. "How are you this morning? Is everything well with you and Señor Barnes?"

Carolyn stopped in front of him. "I'm sure everything is fine," she answered, though the frown remained. "It's just . . . Actually, I was wondering if you've seen Julia this morning."

Ramon raised his eyebrows, his heart skipping a beat at the question. "I haven't, no. Have you?"

Carolyn shook her head, her short gray curls scarcely moving. "I haven't either. At first I thought she was just sleeping late since there was no school today. But I've knocked on her door several times now, and she doesn't answer." She glanced around the compound before returning her gaze to

Ramon. "I can't find her anywhere. I was hoping she might have stopped in to talk with you."

An icy chill slithered up Ramon's spine and settled in around his neck and shoulders. He didn't like the sound of this. He swallowed. "Have you looked . . . everywhere?"

"Everywhere. I don't know where else to look. I was on my way to get Frank when I saw you." She lowered her voice. "You don't think . . . Do you suppose she might have left the compound?"

The chill became an iron grip around his throat. He forced himself to swallow in hopes of breaking it. "I . . . I pray not. We've warned her, but . . ."

Carolyn's dark eyes narrowed. "But she may not have realized how dangerous it could be for her out there . . . alone."

The horror of finding his wife's remains on the jungle floor washed over him, and his knees nearly buckled. "We must find her. Quickly."

Carolyn nodded. "Come with me. We'll get Frank."

In moments they had alerted Frank, and they decided to head out immediately as a group, searching the nearby forest first and then moving on into town. "We all know it won't do any good to try to enlist local authorities from Chamula," Frank said. "They don't even recognize Mexican law and allow no outside police or military forces into their town. They have their own police force, sure, but they're not about to help us locate someone they don't want here in the first place." He shook his head as he looked from Ramon to Carolyn and back. "But first, before we take one step outside these walls, we need to pray. God knows exactly where Julia is, and only He can keep her safe and lead us to her." He reached out his hands, and the three of them joined in a small prayer circle. "Padre, will you lead us?"

Ramon swallowed again, trying to chase away the fear that blocked his ability to think or speak. Señor Barnes was right. They must pray and trust God before taking even one step on their own. The lovely Julia's life might very well depend on it, and he couldn't imagine the pain of dealing with yet another loss of such a fine woman.

"Father . . ." The word nearly stuck in his throat, as tears threatened to flow from his closed eyes. "Father, please, You know our hearts, our concerns, our fears. And we know Your faithfulness and Your great love for each of us, including Señora Bennington. You know everything about her—where she is, what is happening to her at this very moment, and what You have purposed for her life. Thank You that we can rest in that and know that You go ahead of us as we leave this place to search for her. Help us to remember, Lord, that Your Word promises that You have not given us a spirit of fear, but of power and love and a sound mind. Please let us operate in that now, as we go out to look for the señora. Go ahead of us, Father, please, and show us the way. And above all, please bring her back to us safely. We ask all this in Your dear Son's name. Amen."

With that the three of them headed for the gate. It was slightly after noon as they stepped onto the dirt road in front of the compound. The sun shone warm overhead as they walked in the direction of town, their eyes darting into the forest and their hearts listening for God's direction.

The Barneses called out "Julia" every few steps, while Ramon called "Señora." But no answer came.

They'd gone only a short distance when an especially thick and colorful stand of ti plants caught Ramon's eye. "Señora Bennington mentioned to me once that she loved the ti plants." He looked toward Carolyn. "Do you think she might have stopped here to look at them?"

Frank and Carolyn exchanged questioning glances. "It's possible," Carolyn said. "She and I have gone into the forest a couple of times—not far, of course—and you're right that these seem to be her favorites."

Frank shrugged. "Then let's go in a little ways and look. We have to start somewhere."

Calling her name repeatedly, the three walked toward the abundant ti plants and past them into the fringes of the forest. But still they heard nothing except the occasional screech of a monkey disturbed by their presence.

They were about to give up and head back to the road when a patch of red caught Ramon's eye near the path where they walked. His heart raced as he stepped toward it, an image of Julia's floral-print shopping bag swirling in his mind. It didn't take long to bend down and confirm that it was exactly what he'd suspected. His anguished cry brought Frank and Carolyn running to his side.

"What is it?" Frank asked, kneeling down to examine Ramon's findings.

It was Carolyn who bent down and took the bag from Ramon's hand, reaching inside to check the contents. Julia's favorite white shawl was the first item she retrieved.

Once again the memories of discovering his wife's decomposing body on the jungle floor clutched Ramon's heart as he allowed the tears to flow down his cheeks. *"Dios mio,"* he sobbed. "My God, my God! We have lost Señora Bennington too!"

★ ★ ★

JULIA LAY ON HER SIDE, frozen in fear, her arms tied behind her and her legs bound at the ankles. The filthy gag in her mouth made it difficult to breathe and impossible to scream, though she doubted it would do any good anyway. Despite the blindfold over her eyes, she knew she'd been kidnapped and thrown into the back of some sort of enclosed vehicle. Each jolt down the bumpy road made her discomfort worse, but her only real concern was that no one knew where she was. How would she ever be rescued? And what did her captor plan to do with her?

The stench of sweat and various other odors she couldn't identify made her stomach roil, but she knew she didn't dare allow herself to vomit with the gag on. She tried to focus on breathing slowly and lying very still, though everything in her wanted to kick and scream and loose herself from her bonds.

Her nose began to itch, and she moved her head so she could scratch her nose against her shoulder. Suddenly she realized she could see a sliver of light below the blindfold. Excited, she began to rub her head against her shoulder until the blindfold had moved high enough to allow her to see with one eye.

She looked around and confirmed that she was indeed lying on the backseat of an old enclosed vehicle—no doubt the one she had heard chugging along behind her as she walked home from town. Why hadn't she paid more attention? More important, why hadn't she heeded the many warnings not to leave the compound by herself?

Tears stung her eyes then, wetting the blindfold. Had her parents and children been right? Should she have stayed home with them, as they'd begged her to do? Worse yet, how would they feel when they heard she'd disappeared? Would her body ever be found? Oh, how foolish she had been to take this ill-advised outing today!

Noises of street activity caught her attention, and she realized they must be passing through San Juan Chamula, possibly near the marketplace where she'd shopped earlier. Oh, if only she could cry out! Would anyone hear her? And if they did, would they bother to try and help?

In that moment she knew she had to try. She summoned every ounce of her strength and pushed herself to a sitting position, careful not to make any noise and alert the driver, whose dark hair was all she could see. She was directly behind him, on the driver's side. She kept her head down below his seat level, praying he wouldn't see her in the rearview mirror. Then she peered out the window just as they passed the tamale vendor where she'd bought her morning meal. No one seemed to notice the passing vehicle, and she despaired of drawing anyone's attention—until she spotted the little girl with the old lady. Was it Itzel? Could it be?

The child looked up as they drove past, and her dark eyes registered surprise and what Julia prayed was recognition. Yes, Itzel had seen her! Did she recognize her with the blindfold and gag on? *Oh, please, Itzel, please, realize it's me and get help!*

As the vehicle jounced past the still-staring girl, Julia could no longer hold back her tears. A sob escaped her aching throat, and she began to weep, her head leaning against the window. A string of curses erupted from the front seat, and the man slammed on his brakes, knocking Julia into the back of the seat.

The meanest face Julia had ever seen—one that might have been attractive if not so hateful—glared at her. Leaning over the console and grabbing her by the hair, her captor yanked her close.

"Do you want to die now, señora, right here in the middle of the road? Because if you do, I will be happy to make that happen." He laughed. "And if you think anyone out there will stop me, you do not know these people well at all." With his spare hand he flashed a knife in front of her face. "I do not want to use this on you, señora—at least, not yet—but I will if I have to." With a thrust that sent her backward against the seat, he loosed her hair and growled, "Now lie down on the seat, and don't move again. *Comprende?*"

Trembling, Julia nodded and lay down, drawing her knees up to her chest as she continued to weep.

★ ★ ★

ITZEL THOUGHT HER LEGS had turned to stone. One minute she'd been walking with her abuela, just about to enter the marketplace, and the next she could no longer move. Her eyes felt as if they would pop from her head. She wanted to scream, wanted to say something, but she could not. She couldn't run, she couldn't talk, she could only stand, staring after the big, white car she'd seen the day before, the one with the mean man driving it. But this time her teacher was in the car too. How could that be?

True, she hadn't been able to see the señora's entire face, but her red curls could belong to no one else. And what little she had seen of the woman's face looked more scared than Itzel herself had ever been, even after one of her worst nightmares.

Why was the señora in the car, and where was that mean man taking her? Questions swirled through her head, even as her abuela grabbed her arm and shook her back from her thoughts.

"What are you doing, Itzel? Stop standing in the road staring. We must finish our shopping and go back home." The woman tugged firmly on Itzel's arm. "Come, Itzel. Now."

Itzel could no longer see the big, white car as she gazed down the road, but some of the dust it had kicked up still remained in the air. She looked up at her grandmother and opened her mouth to speak. But what? What would she say?

She closed her mouth and swallowed, then hung her head and put one foot in front of the other, trudging after her abuela as she wrestled with the fear in her heart and the thoughts in her head that made no sense.

★ CHAPTER 19 ★

HERNANDO REMINDED HIMSELF NOT TO SPEED. He needed to look like anyone else on the road, coming and going without any care or urgency. But he couldn't wait to get back to San Cristobal de las Casas, back to the ugly casita where his three compadres and one bad-tempered dog waited for him. He had told no one where he was going or what he hoped to accomplish, but he had succeeded beyond his wildest dreams. At best he'd hoped to locate one or both of the Americanas from the compound and maybe learn enough about them to figure out the best way to get them alone and grab them. He smirked as he continued down the road toward home. The stupid gringa had made his job so easy he could hardly believe it.

He glanced in the rearview mirror, which he had now adjusted so he could keep an eye on her. It was obvious she was shaking and crying, but at least she was no longer trying to summon help through the window—as if that would have worked. People around here kept to themselves, especially when it came to strangers who weren't welcome in the first place.

Hernando took one last look at her red curls before returning his eyes to the road. He'd always been attracted to redheaded women, and even though this one was nearly old enough to be his mother, she was well preserved—not like some of the old hags who lived around here and looked ancient before they were forty. Yes, he would enjoy this one before concluding the financial business concerning her. And if her family couldn't or wouldn't come up with the ransom, he would make sure he recouped his losses through personal pleasures before slitting her throat and leaving her body to rot on the jungle floor.

He shook his head and grinned, thinking of how stunned he had been to spot her leaving the marketplace and heading in the direction of the compound. He hadn't realized how close the compound was and thought he'd lost his chance to grab her when he rounded that last bend and saw that she had almost reached her destination. Then she'd veered off into the rain forest, no doubt to admire the colorful plants and flowers. He laughed again. She had practically sent him an invitation—and he had gladly accepted.

Wait until his compadres saw the prize he had brought home! His grin faded, though, when he realized he might have competition for the woman's favors.

No way. I found her, and I took her. Until her family pays the ransom, she's mine. Nobody touches her but me! I will personally guard her, and even sleep out there with her. No one gets to her except over my dead body.

The thought gave him serious pause, for he knew none of his compadres would think twice about killing him if he had something they wanted badly enough. He would therefore have to be especially careful to make sure that didn't happen.

★ ★ ★

MARIE HAD ALTERNATED BETWEEN PRAYING and crying for most of the day, though she did her best to hide her distress in front of her husband and grandchildren. Brittney had returned midafternoon from her Black Friday shopping, declaring that she was never going to get sucked into such a crazy practice again. Marie imagined the girl's resolve would last until this time next year.

Together they had oohed and aahed over what Brittney considered her "killer" purchases, and then they had worked together in the kitchen to heat up leftovers for the four of them. Marie finally managed to snag the men from in front of the television and plunk them down at the dining room table long enough for dinner.

She watched them eat and told herself how blessed they all were to be together, despite the fact that Julia wasn't here with them. They seemed to be enjoying themselves as they loaded their plates with second helpings, while Marie struggled to get down just a few bites of the tiny portions she had taken for herself.

I just wish I knew what was going on with Julia. I hate that their phone service is so spotty down there, but I'm going to try and give them a call after dinner anyway. Even if I can't get through to Julia on her cell, I can at least try to reach Carolyn and Frank on their landline. At least that seems to work most of the time.

With that resolution to tide her over, Marie managed to get through dinner. When John and Tyler returned to the family room to watch more football and Brittney offered to clean up the kitchen, Marie didn't argue. She immediately went to her room and closed the door behind her.

Three tries to Julia's cell phone went straight to voice mail. Julia had told her that most of the time she didn't even have it on, so Marie wasn't too surprised. She thumbed through her address book, found the Barneses' number, picked up her own landline, and dialed.

The first call didn't go through, but after her second try rang several times, a hesitant male voice answered. Marie recognized the voice as belonging to Frank Barnes, but he didn't sound like his usual welcoming self. The alarm that had been buzzing in the background of Marie's mind most of the day suddenly grew louder.

"Frank? Is that you? This is Marie Lawson."

The pause lasted so long Marie was beginning to think she'd lost her connection. At last Frank answered.

"Marie, yes, it's me. Frank. I . . ." His voice trailed off, and she thought she heard him take a deep breath before he continued. "Carolyn and I were just thinking we should call you, but we were waiting, hoping it wouldn't be necessary."

This time the silence of his pause slammed into her ears in a way that buckled her knees. She sat down on the rocker beside her bed. Whatever Frank was about to tell her was something she did not want to hear.

"Marie, I . . . I don't know how to tell you this. There just isn't any easy way to do it. It . . . it's about Julia. She's . . . missing."

★ ★ ★

THE FIRST THING Hernando noticed when he pulled up in front of the rundown house he and his compadres now called home was how ludicrous the sleek, black Mercedes appeared. It sat in the driveway like it owned the place, and the bolt of fear that shot up Hernando's spine confirmed that its owner very well might.

He swallowed, wondering how best to handle the situation. If he were alone, he'd just walk in and see what happened. But he had a woman with him—bound, gagged, and crying. He knew the visitor had been sent by his boss, and obtaining ransom money was what they'd been pushing for, so if he handled things right, this could go well for him. If he didn't . . . well, that wasn't an option. He would do what he had to do, but what about the woman? She would certainly be easier to handle if she were quiet. Did he dare threaten her and hope she'd cooperate? Even gagged, the woman could become hysterical and create a scene.

He cursed the timing. What he really wanted to do was pull into the driveway, past the house and into the backyard where he could take her straight to the back shed where they'd kept their previous captives. Once he had her tied up there, she would be no problem. The last thing he needed to do was risk being seen bringing her into the house through the front door. Even if no one spotted them, their visitor wouldn't take kindly to his taking such a chance.

There was only one solution. He would have to tie her more securely, with her arms and legs trussed up behind her so she couldn't possibly cause any problems. He'd reinforce her gag and blindfold and then go inside and deal with the situation before removing his hostage from the vehicle.

This was going to make his resolution to keep the woman to himself a bit harder to enforce, but he was determined to find a way. He wasn't about to alter his plans for the attractive redhead in the backseat.

★ CHAPTER 20 ★

EL TORO WAS ONLY two steps below El Jefe himself. Hernando had met him before and understood why he was called "the bull." Well over six feet tall, his massive frame filled a doorway, and his arm muscles bulged under his loose-fitting white cotton shirt. To call him intimidating was an understatement; and though Hernando would use wisdom in conversing with him, he wasn't about to back down.

"El Toro," he said as he stepped into the kitchen and spotted the visitor sitting at the table with Raul and their other two roommates. El Toro's two nameless assistants, who accompanied him everywhere, stood silently behind their boss. "It is good to see you again, *amigo.*"

The man's lids lowered over his dark eyes, as he glared at Hernando. "Amigo? Who said we were friends? I am not here on a social visit. El Jefe has sent me to check on you."

Hernando felt his sweat glands kick into overdrive, as rivulets of perspiration began to drip down his back and under his arms. *"Lo siento,* El Toro. I'm sorry. I didn't mean to imply that you are here on a social visit. I understand the reason for your visit, and I welcome it. I have good news for you."

The beefy man lifted his heavy eyebrows. "Sí? And what would that good news be?"

Hernando resisted the impulse to swallow. He knew how important it was to mask his discomfort. El Toro was better at sniffing out fear than Bruno, and nearly as fast at responding to it. Forcing himself to speak in a clear, steady voice, he said, "I have just returned from San Juan Chamula, where I located an Americana who lives in the La Paz Compound. It is easy to see she is from a family with money and that she has good breeding."

The man's eyebrows lifted higher. "So where is this American woman of good breeding? How soon can you take her and begin the ransom proceedings?"

Despite his efforts at appearing confident and unafraid, Hernando felt his face flush. He had hoped to move the woman straight from the Blazer to the back room before announcing her presence to the others. Obviously that was no longer an option.

"I . . . I have already taken her. She is in the back of my Blazer right now, tied up and gagged and blindfolded."

Surprise registered on El Toro's face, but only for a brief moment. His eyebrows lowered and drew into a frown. "And why have you left her out there? Why have you not moved her inside?"

"I had intended to do that," Hernando answered, trying to ignore the thumping tattoo of his heart against his ribs. "But I need to drive past the house to the back, where I can transfer her to the shed without risk of being seen."

El Toro's head scarcely moved, but Hernando was certain he had nodded. "And you need me to move my car so you can do that."

"Sí, El Toro."

Hernando waited, continuing to perspire but managing to hold himself still and his gaze steady.

The bear of a man stood to his feet, nearly knocking over the flimsy chair in the process. He reached into his pants pocket and produced a set of keys, which he handed to one of his assistants, even as his eyes remained fixed on Hernando. "Move my car," he ordered. "After Hernando has pulled the Blazer into the yard, move my car back. I do not want it left on the street. There is not one scratch on it now, and I intend to keep it that way."

Wordlessly the assistant took the keys and immediately went outside, with Hernando following close behind.

★ ★ ★

MARIE COULD SCARCELY HEAR her own thoughts above the buzzing in her ears. The sound had started when Frank told her Julia was missing, and it had elevated throughout their brief conversation. Frank had tried to reassure her and had eventually put Carolyn on the phone to try to help calm Marie's fears, but it hadn't worked. Marie had done enough research on the area to know that the compound was located on the outskirts of San Juan Chamula, a primarily Mayan community that did not welcome strangers and did not allow the Mexican military or police to intervene in what they considered their own private affairs. Anything that took place within the greater San Juan Chamula area qualified, meaning that no one was going to help the Barneses locate Julia.

Carolyn had reassured her that she, Frank, and Padre Ramon were going back out to search for Julia in a matter of moments. They'd come back to the compound to retrieve jackets and flashlights, but they'd already located Julia's shopping bag on the fringe of the rain forest, so they had a good idea where to look.

"She'll probably turn up any minute," Carolyn said, "even if we don't find her. I imagine she just lost track of the time."

Marie didn't believe her, but she thanked her anyway and made her promise to let them know the minute they found her. *Alive, please, Lord!* she'd prayed silently as she hung up the phone.

As she made her way down the stairs from her room, she asked herself how she would possibly deliver this news to her husband and grandchildren. And yet she knew she must. Not only did they have a right to know, but she and John needed to pray together. Maybe Tyler and Brittney would even join in.

She made a mental note to call the prayer chain at church, and then took a deep breath and went to the kitchen to retrieve Brittney, who was finishing her cleanup work.

"Hey, Grandma, I'm just about done here." Her welcoming smile faded when their eyes met. "What's wrong? Are you OK? You look pale."

Marie stepped up to her granddaughter and took her hand. "Come into the family room with me. I need to tell you all something."

The girl's eyes widened. "It's Mom, isn't it? Something happened to Mom."

"Please, honey. I'll tell you when we're all together."

Tears popped into Brittney's eyes, but she nodded and followed her into the family room, where the TV blasted reruns of highlights from the major bowl games. It took a moment to get the men's attention.

John frowned when he saw the two women standing side by side in the doorway. "What is it? What happened?"

Marie wasn't surprised that she hadn't had to say a thing before her husband recognized there was a problem. They had been married for decades, and there wasn't much they didn't know about one another.

"It's Julia," she said, this time snagging Tyler's attention as well.

John reached for the remote and shut off the TV as Marie and Brittney went to the couch and sat down beside him. Tyler sat up straight in the adjacent recliner and leaned forward, his elbows on his knees. "Is Mom OK? Did something happen to her?"

Marie swallowed. "I don't know. She's . . . missing."

Tyler was the first to react. "Missing?" He jumped to his feet. "How can she be missing? I thought she lived and worked in a walled compound. How can someone go missing in a place like that?"

John reached up and laid a hand on Tyler's arm. "Take it easy, son. I'm sure there's more to the story." Tyler waited quietly then, but he did not retake his seat.

"Not much more," Marie admitted. "It seems they had all warned Julia many times never to leave the compound alone, but they believe that's what she must have done. They found her shopping bag full of items from the marketplace, so apparently she decided to go to town and do a little shopping."

"Shopping?" This time it was John who reacted. "What in the world kind of shopping could be so urgent that she'd leave the safety of the compound and go out into that heathen environment on her own? What could she have been thinking?" He squinted at his wife then. "And just where did they find this shopping bag?"

Marie shook her head slightly, knowing the answer would only make the situation worse. But she had to tell them. They deserved to know. "It was . . . just inside the rain forest, not far from the compound. Frank and Carolyn believe she must have been on her way back from town when she decided to stop and check out some plants or flowers or something."

Silence hung in the air. At last Tyler broke it. "She went into the jungle . . . alone?" His dark eyes watered, and Marie could tell he was on the edge of breaking down. "So what happened to her? Why would she leave her shopping bag behind, unless . . ."

His voice trailed off as he gave words to the question that no doubt danced through all their minds. Why would she leave her shopping bag behind, indeed? It certainly couldn't have been of her own free will. Carolyn had told her there were no signs of blood in the area, which they imagined there would be if Julia had been attacked by an animal. Besides, the animals seldom came that close to the edge of the forest, preferring to stay hidden within its familiar depths.

But if not an animal, then what?

"So what about the police?" Brittney asked, brushing away tears as she looked from one grandparent to the other. "What do they think happened?"

Marie shot up a silent prayer as she handed out yet one more piece of this frightening puzzle. "Basically there are no police in San Juan Chamula—at least not any that extend their efforts to what they consider strangers or intruders to their way of life. The town is made up primarily of people of Mayan ancestry, and they greatly resent anyone they see as threatening what's left of their old way of life. Julia would . . ." She swallowed a sob. "She would definitely fit into that category."

Tyler's face reddened. "So they're doing nothing? No one's trying to find Mom?"

"The Barneses are, of course, and the pastor from the compound. They've been searching for her most of the afternoon, but there's a lot of ground to cover and they had to come back for flashlights so they could continue looking in the dark." Marie knew even as she spoke the words that what should be an assurance only deepened their despair. If they hadn't found her by now, what were the chances they ever would?

"I knew it," Tyler exploded, beginning to pace the length of the room. "I knew we shouldn't have let her go." He glared at Brittney. "I told you, Britt! First we lose Dad, and now Mom. I can't believe this. I can't believe any of it." He raked his hand through his dark hair, and John got up to approach him.

"Tyler, none of us wanted her to go, but it was her decision. Now we stick together and pray for her safety. It's the only thing we can do, son."

He tried to gather the boy into his arms, but Tyler pulled away. "Pray? Are you kidding me? Why would I ask God for a favor when all He's done for me lately is take away people I love?" He shook his head. "No way. If you all want to pray, fine. But count me out." His gaze moved from one to the other before coming to rest on his grandfather. "I think we need to go down there. Now. Tonight. As soon as we can. We've got to find her."

Marie watched the myriad of emotions cross her husband's face, and she knew he too wished he could be there, actively searching for his daughter. He also knew how pointless it would be. Better to trust that to people who knew the area and the local customs. Prayer truly was the only—as well as the best—course of action, even if neither grandchild joined them. Marie knew that she and her husband needed to begin praying immediately and not give up until they had an answer. And how she hoped it would be an answer they could live with!

★ ★ ★

JULIA MOANED. Every muscle in her body ached. The kidnapping itself had been terrifying enough, but then she'd been spirited away in a vehicle by some man she didn't know and for what purpose she had no idea—and didn't even want to imagine. She'd been tied, blindfolded, and gagged, and then after a bone-jostling ride had been trussed up even tighter while her captor apparently left the vehicle for some reason.

And then he'd come back, moved the vehicle a very short distance, and untied her just enough that he could lead her into some sort of room, where she'd then been tied to a rough, hard chair. At first she'd been confident that she and her captor were the only ones in the room, but soon she'd heard other voices—two or three of them, at least. And a dog, one with a growl that made her skin crawl.

Oh, why had she left the compound alone? Why hadn't she waited until Carolyn could join her? There was no guarantee they wouldn't both have been taken, but surely it would have been less likely. And, of course, her biggest mistake was venturing into the forest when she had been so close to La Paz. A few more steps and she would have been safe. Would that last mistake prove to be a fatal one?

She tried to focus on the conversation near her, all of it spoken in Spanish. The way they spoke assured her that they were most likely Mexican people and not Mayans, but that knowledge offered her little comfort. She already knew the Mayans didn't like outsiders, but it was obvious that her non-Mayan captors did not have any sort of altruistic plans for her either.

"How did you find her?" one voice asked. "And how do you know her family has money?"

"El Toro, I . . . we . . . heard of her in Chamula—of two Americanas, actually. But when I went back to try to learn more about them and how I might find them, I spotted this one by herself. She fit the description of one of the two women perfectly, including her red hair. I heard she was from America and worked at the compound. We all know those Americanas come to places like this for only one reason—to feel better about themselves because they have so much while others have so little." The man laughed, and the sound of it slithered up Julia's spine. "She made it so easy for me when she went into the jungle alone."

Deep-throated laughter from several others confirmed her suspicions that she was the only female in the room, and that there were at least three or four others, maybe more, all discussing her plight in a way that served only to reinforce her terror. *Have I been kidnapped? Am I being held for ransom?* She had wondered about that since the moment she'd been bound and tossed into the man's vehicle. In some ways that was better than the possibility that the man had taken her to rape or kill her, though even being held for ransom didn't preclude those possibilities or guarantee her safe rescue. *How much will they ask for? My parents don't have much, and my children have nothing. Oh, if only they would remove this awful gag so I could explain that to them.*

The one she'd heard referred to as El Toro spoke next. "Let us hope you are right, Hernando. You cannot afford another mistake, even a small one. El Jefe has instructed me to remind you of that fact. You would do well to get the information you need to send the ransom demand. How much will you ask, and how quickly do you think you can produce it?"

The voice belonging to the one she now identified as Hernando responded. "For a woman like her, so beautiful and so high-class? I think her family must be very rich and they will want her back quickly. Who wouldn't? She is quite a prize, as you can see. I believe I will ask for a million dollars. And why not? She is worth it, no?"

"I hope you are right, Hernando," the one called El Toro replied. "If they think half as highly of her as you seem to, they will pay up immediately. But a million might be more than we can hope for. If they offer half a million, take it, but not a dime less. Understand, amigo?"

El Toro's tone dripped with sarcasm as he emphasized the word for friend. Julia quickly surmised that they were anything but. The revelation, however, was nearly lost in the horror of the amount she now knew would be asked for her ransom. Even if her parents mortgaged their home, she doubted they could raise that sort of money.

I'm going to die here—alone and without my family. I'll never be able to tell them how much I love them or how sorry I am for causing them such pain.

Despite the blindfold and gag, tears formed in her eyes and she began to sob, not caring if she suffocated in the process. She was going to die anyway, so why not do it now, before these horrible men employed whatever means they might come up with to get her to give them her family's contact information? If it came to that, she hoped she'd be able to hold out. Why drag her parents and children into this when there was absolutely nothing they could do to help her?

Once again the thought came that she should never have left the compound alone that morning, but it was too late for regrets. It seemed her fate was sealed.

★ CHAPTER 21 ★

RAMON FELT AS IF HE WERE BATTLING the very powers of darkness as he swept his flashlight beam from left to right, and then back again, ever so slowly making his way across the patch of ground he'd agreed to search. The Barneses and a couple of others from the compound were searching their own areas, but all had agreed to stay within shouting distance of one another.

"Julia!"

"Señora Bennington!"

Calls went out from someone in the group every few seconds, but so far without response. More than once tears had welled in Ramon's eyes, but he quickly brushed them away. He had to focus on finding Señora Bennington; he would give vent to his emotions later.

Please, El Señor, please let her be all right. You know where she is, Lord. Keep her safe, and show us how to find her!

The padre imagined that the others in the group uttered similar prayers, either silently or aloud, as they searched, but he knew this was more personal for him. Not only did it bring back memories of the wife he lost in this very rain forest years ago, but it confronted his denial that he cared more for Julia Bennington than he wanted to admit.

I have no right, he reminded himself. *True, we are both alone, having lost our spouses, but that does not put me in a position to court such a one as Señora Bennington. She is from a fine family in the United States; I am but a simple pastor without even a home to call my own. She is here to teach the children for one school year, nothing more. Even if we find her and she is all right, the best I can hope for is that she will stay and finish her teaching commitment and then go home. I will probably never hear from her again.*

It occurred to him then that he had used the word *if* in regard to finding Julia Bennington alive and well. He'd known from the moment he'd heard of her disappearance that they might never find her again—or if they did, she might not be alive—but he was not yet ready to contemplate that possibility. He shoved it from his mind and resumed his search—and his prayers.

★ ★ ★

TYLER KNEW IT WAS POINTLESS TO TRY TO SLEEP, but he simply could not remain in the family room with the others once his grandparents sat down together, clasped hands, and began to pray. Even Brittney had joined in, though silently, with her head bowed. Tyler imagined his sister needed to be close to her grandparents and draw from whatever hope and comfort they found in praying to a God who probably didn't even exist, let alone listen, but that was her choice. Personally, he would have no part of it. He might be a lot of things, but he wasn't a hypocrite.

One thing I am, he thought, as he lay in the dark, staring at a nearly invisible ceiling, *is mad. Just plain mad! I told Mom not to go. I practically begged her! But she wouldn't listen. Grandma and Grandpa didn't like it either, but they let her do it. And Brittney defended her so-called right to make her own decisions. What right did Mom have to make a decision that could end like this? We're impacted too. Shouldn't we have had something to say about it?*

The landline rang then, and he popped out of bed. Maybe they'd found her. Maybe his mother was safe after all.

Not even bothering to slip into his flip-flops, he charged out the door and down the stairs just in time to see his grandfather hang up the kitchen phone.

Tyler's heart raced at the implications of such a short call. "Is she OK?" he demanded. "Did they find her?"

His grandfather turned, a look of sadness on his face that made him appear even older than usual. He shook his head. "Nothing. It wasn't about your mom. Just a telemarketer."

Tyler cursed, something he was careful never to do around his grandparents, but his grandpa didn't reprimand him or even shoot him a disappointed look. He simply came over to him and held out his arms. Feeling much like the little boy who had spent countless hours in this man's arms, Tyler accepted the offer. Enfolded in one another's embrace, they stood in the kitchen and cried.

★ ★ ★

HERNANDO BREATHED A HUGE SIGH of relief when El Toro and the others returned to the house, leaving him alone at last with his attractive captive. He would be careful not to put his personal plans into action until he was sure El Toro was gone, but it wouldn't hurt to start working on getting the information he needed to contact her family.

With Bruno on alert just inside the closed doorway, Hernando knelt down beside the red-haired woman. He could smell her fear, and he had no doubt the dog could as well. One brief command would set Bruno on her, and she wouldn't have a chance. But that was not his purpose for this woman. Not only did he want to keep her alive so he could collect the ransom money and turn it over to El Jefe, hopefully reinstating him in the man's good graces once again, but he wanted to enjoy her while he waited. She had no idea how lucky she was that these two factors were in play, or she wouldn't have a prayer of survival.

"Are you comfortable, *cara?*" he whispered, adding the endearment for effect. She had responded to his commands in Spanish before, so he knew she understood him.

The woman didn't answer, but she stopped her whimpering. Good! They had connected.

"I do not wish to hurt you, señora," Hernando crooned, though he imagined he might before all this was over. "I just want to ask you some questions. Simple questions, really. Things you can answer with no problem. If you will do that, we will get along just fine, and soon you will be able to go back to the compound, where I know you wish you were right now." He leaned closer to her ear. "Would you like that, señora?"

Trembling, she nodded.

"Good. Then we understand each other. Now, I am going to take your gag off so you can speak to me. You won't do anything foolish, like screaming for help, will you?"

She shook her head no, her red curls bouncing slightly. He smiled at the sight, anticipating how those curls would feel when he grasped them in his hand. Trying to block out the thoughts that followed, he removed her gag, pleased to see that for a middle-aged woman, she still had full lips.

She didn't say a word, though he noticed her tense up. Good! He would keep her off-balance, guessing what would come next, hoping for the best but anticipating the worst. Hernando loved being in charge.

"Very good, *preciosa*," he whispered, adding another endearment. "You are doing very well. Now, let's keep that up, shall we? We will start with a very simple question. What is your name? And remember, I know you are from the La Paz Compound, so I can find out from other resources if I need to, but why not keep it simple? There is no sense in upsetting me, right?" He leaned yet closer, so close that he felt her shiver when he spoke. "Some people say I'm not very nice when I get upset. I would hate for you to think badly of me." He placed a hand on the back of her neck, squeezing just enough to make her uncomfortable. "So, señora, will you be a good girl and tell me what I want to know, or will we play games until I find out?"

★ CHAPTER 22 ★

JULIA THOUGHT SHE'D NEVER BEEN so terrified in her entire life, not even when Tom had his heart attack. Her resolve to remain strong and give them no information evaporated the instant the horrible man laid his hand on her neck and began to squeeze. The pain wasn't unbearable, but the size of his hand and the strength she felt convinced her that she had no chance against him. It seemed the advantages were all one-sided. Perhaps her only hope for survival—slim as it might be—was to buy some time and pray that somehow, someway she would be rescued.

By whom, she couldn't imagine, but Itzel had seen her . . . hadn't she? Yes, she had seen her, but did she recognize her? And even if she did, would she tell anyone? It was a fragile hope, at best, but Julia needed something to cling to.

Determined to be honest and forthright while revealing only what was necessary to keep from "upsetting" him, she opened her mouth and tried to speak. Her throat was dry, and her lips felt nearly numb from the tight gag she'd worn for several hours now, but she forced herself to speak. "Julia," she croaked. "My name is Julia."

She'd had but one brief look at her captor's face, but she could nearly imagine him sneering as he answered, his mouth still near her ear. "Julia. A beautiful name for a beautiful señora. I like it. It fits you. Julia. I can almost taste its sweetness in my mouth."

She shuddered, and he laughed in response. "Ah, Señora Julia, it seems you look forward to our time together nearly as much as I do." He kissed the tip of her earlobe then. "If you make it worth my while, Señora Julia, perhaps I will not hurt you quite so much." He laughed again, and her stomach churned. Even if by some miracle she made it out of this alive, it was obvious she wouldn't do so unscathed.

"All right then, Señora Julia," the man continued, and she could tell he had stood to his feet and moved away from her side to look directly down at her from the front. "You have done good to tell me your first name, but no doubt you have a last, do you not?" Suddenly he was in her face, breathing his foul breath directly on her as he grabbed the front of her blouse and pulled her close. "Do not play with me, señora. I want your full name. All of it. Right now. And I want to know who you are, where you're from, what you do. Do you understand, señora?"

Her full bladder, combined with her ever-increasing fear, caused her to lose control. Humiliated as well as terrified, she now sat in a warm puddle of her own urine, as tears coursed down her cheeks. "My name is . . . Julia Lawson . . . Bennington," she said between sobs. "I'm from . . . Temecula, California. I'm a . . . widow. I teach high school English. I have . . . two children in college. I . . ."

Julia's words drifted off now, as the reality of how much she had already revealed flooded her thoughts. If she caved this easily, this quickly, how much more would she do or say in an effort to keep him from hurting her?

"Julia Lawson Bennington. A very nice name, señora. You were very wise to reveal this information to me. Of course, we have much more to discuss, but first we must clean you up. I can't have you sitting there all wet and uncomfortable, can I?" He let go of her blouse. "No, I cannot. I am a gentleman, after all, so I will allow you to clean yourself. You understand, though, that I must watch to be sure you don't try anything foolish."

The implications of his words hit Julia like a fist in the stomach, even as he began to untie her. When both her feet and one hand were free, he gripped her arm and squeezed until she moaned. "Do not think of trying to escape, señora." He pricked the skin on her neck with what she was sure was a knife. She felt a trickle of warm blood run down into her collarbone. "This knife is my enforcer, and I keep it by my side at all times. Do you understand?"

Her blindfold was damp with tears by that time, but she nodded. It would be pointless to fight him anyway. *Oh God, help me,* she begged silently. *Please help me!*

Before long she found herself once again sitting on the hard wooden chair, but this time stripped and still blindfolded. Using a damp cloth he'd given her, she tried as best she could to clean herself. Throughout the procedure, which he encouraged her to drag out for reasons she didn't even want to contemplate, he hummed and laughed and spoke various endearments to her, promising they would get to know each other much better as time went on. He was able to restrain himself from doing more only because he knew that El Toro or one of his men could return at any moment.

When she was finished, Hernando wrapped her in a scratchy wool blanket that smelled like a dog, no doubt the one she'd heard growling off and on. She hoped the dog wouldn't be angry that she'd been given his blanket. But as her captor retied her to the chair, she realized she wasn't going to be raped after all—at least not right now. That brought some sense of relief, but from the sound of his promises for the future, she imagined it wouldn't be long.

"There," he said, adjusting the blindfold that had remained in place while she cleaned herself. "You are now clean once again. You know, señora, if you had been patient, I would have given you a chance to relieve yourself properly. Keep that in mind for next time, will you?" He leaned down close to her. "Unless, of course, you would like me to wash you. I would be happy to do so any time you wish."

Repulsed, she pulled back as far as the straight-backed chair would allow. She despised this man, hated him in a way she'd never imagined she could hate anyone. But her fear of him was greater even than her hatred. He was an evil man, and he had complete control of her. What would he do next?

"I have been thinking, cara," he said, apparently sitting in front of her now. "It's been a long day, and you must be very hungry. Would you like me to get you something to eat?"

Julia realized she hadn't eaten since the tiny breakfast she'd purchased at the marketplace that morning. It seemed ages ago, though it was undoubtedly only hours. How many? She had no idea. And under normal conditions she would certainly be hungry by now. But these were not normal conditions, and the thought of food set her stomach to churning again.

Did she dare refuse his offer? Would that be the thing that upset him and caused him to be "not so nice," as he'd warned?

She swallowed. "That would be . . . nice. Thank you."

The man laughed. "Ah, so the señora is either very hungry or very smart." She smelled his body odor again as he leaned so close their foreheads touched. "I think it is not hunger that drives you, so you must be smart, eh? You said you were a teacher, after all. All right, smart lady, here is what you must do if you wish to eat—not just now but ever again. Give me the names of your family, those who care enough to pay money to get you back. You said you are a widow, so there is no husband, but there are others, yes? Of course there are. You mentioned two children in college. And your parents . . . what about them? I imagine they will pay whatever I ask to get their precious Señora Julia Lawson Bennington back, safe and sound. Am I right?"

Denials and explanations swirled through her mind, but she sensed he would not receive them well. Still, she had to at least make one attempt to dissuade him from asking the impossible. "My family has no money—not much, anyway. My children are in college, and my parents are elderly."

He pressed his forehead harder against hers. "They own a home, don't they? Everyone in the United States owns a home. You do also, yes?"

Tears once again pricked her eyes. "Yes."

"Very good. And what about when your husband died? Surely he left you a big insurance policy."

The policy Tom had left was far from large and had long since been used to help pay college tuition for Tyler and Brittney, but she knew the man did not want to hear that. "Yes," was all she whispered.

"Very good, señora." He pulled back from her. "Now, what are your parents' names, and how do I reach them?"

★ ★ ★

WHEN THE PHONE RANG in the middle of the night, Marie shot up to a sitting position, eyes wide open and heart racing. It wasn't that the ringing had awakened her, as she'd done nothing but toss and turn, pray and cry, since she and John had come to bed a little before midnight. She was almost certain Tyler and Brittney weren't sleeping either, but somehow John had managed to drift off.

She grabbed the receiver from the stand beside the bed, fully aware that any call at that hour couldn't be good news. But in this case, wasn't it possible? Wasn't there at least a chance that it was Carolyn or Frank Barnes calling to say they'd found Julia and she was all right?

"Hello?" Her voice sounded more like a desperate cry than a greeting.

By that time John had switched on the light beside the bed and he was sitting up beside her, an anxious look on his face. "Who is it?" he whispered.

She shushed him with a wave of her hand, straining to hear the voice at the other end, praying it was indeed good news.

"Señora Lawson?" a man's voice asked.

Marie swallowed. "Yes. Who is this?"

"It is not important who I am. What is important is that your daughter is here with me. And she is safe . . . for the moment."

Marie gasped and John snatched the phone from her hand. "Who is this?" he demanded.

Marie watched as John listened, his face going pale. She saw his jaw twitch. Whatever the man was telling him, it wasn't good.

"But that's . . . that's impossible," John said. "We don't have that kind of money."

He listened again, and this time she saw tears pop into his hazel eyes. She shivered next to him.

Finally, after only a few brief words of ascent from John, he hung up. He raised his eyes to hers and shook his head. "They want a million dollars. A million dollars, Marie. Where are we going to get that kind of money?"

Marie felt her eyes widen. "What are you talking about? Who wants a million dollars?"

"The people who kidnapped our daughter. They said we have three days. Then he'll call us again and tells us where to wire the money. Three days! It might as well be three years."

The reality of his words were beginning to sink into Marie's heart, as well as her mind, and she felt herself trembling. "What will happen if we don't send it?"

His jaw twitched again. "He said . . ." A sob escaped before he could finish. "He said we will get Julia back either way, but if we don't pay the money, it will be in pieces."

A cry escaped Marie's lips, and she fell into John's arms. By that time Brittney and Tyler had come to the door and were waiting for an explanation.

"Was that call about Mom?" Tyler asked, standing in the open doorway in his pajama bottoms and a white T-shirt, with Brittney peering over his shoulder. Both looked like frightened children.

John nodded and patted the foot of the bed. "Yes, it was about your mom. Come and sit down, both of you. Please."

★ ★ ★

ITZEL PULLED THE COVER OVER HER HEAD and tried to cry silently, but the house was so small that it was only a few minutes before her abuela came to sit on her sleeping mat.

"What is it, Itzel?" The old woman pulled the covers back and peered down at her. Itzel knew her abuela could see her because the moonlight shone through the window, and Itzel could see the frown on her abuela's face.

Itzel swallowed. "It is nothing, Abuela. I . . . I had a bad dream."

The grandmother nodded, and her forehead smoothed out. "Bad dreams. Yes, children have them often." She shrugged. "Old people too, like me." Her frown returned. "But never do I cry about them, and I have never heard you do so either. So what is the real reason you are crying?" She leaned down slightly. "Do not lie to me, little one."

Itzel sighed. No matter how hard she tried, she never seemed able to hide anything from her abuela. This would be no different.

"When we went back to the marketplace today, I . . . saw something."

"What did you see?"

Itzel swallowed. "I saw a mean man. I saw him yesterday too."

The old woman looked surprised now. "And how do you know he is mean?"

"His face. He looks very mean. And he says bad words."

Abuela nodded. "So, he is a mean man. Is that what scared you and made you cry? Do you think he will hurt you?"

Itzel imagined he might if he could, but that wasn't why she was crying. She shook her head. "No. I am crying because he had my teacher in his car."

This time the old woman looked genuinely confused. "What do you mean, Itzel? Are you talking about your teacher from La Paz? She was with this mean man?"

Itzel nodded. "Yes. But I do not believe she wanted to be there. She had a rag in her mouth and something over her eyes."

Frowning once again, the abuela sat up straight. "You are not making sense. I think you are making this up."

"No!" Itzel's protest came out as a cry, and she dissolved into tears. "I am not . . . making this up," she protested between sobs. "The mean man has . . . taken my . . . teacher away. "

The old woman gathered the child into her arms. "I do not understand what you are saying, little one, but we will talk about this more in the morning. For now you must get some sleep."

Itzel doubted that sleep was possible, but she would honor her abuela's wishes and try. Surely tomorrow, when they talked about it again, her abuela would know what to do.

★ CHAPTER 23 ★

RAMON AWOKE WITH A JOLT to the sound of pounding on his door. He was shocked to realize he'd finally fallen asleep, even if it had been in his chair beside his bed. The last he remembered was when he and the Barneses agreed to catch a few hours of sleep and resume their efforts in the morning. He had returned home and sat down to pray for a few minutes before going to bed. Apparently that's as far as he'd gotten.

The light was just beginning to penetrate the window, so he knew it was still early. The pounding continued, along with Frank Barnes's voice calling his name.

His head cleared now, he rushed to the door and yanked it open. Surely this meant that Julia had returned or they at least had good news. But the look on Frank's face told him otherwise.

"What is it?" he asked, as he stepped back so his friend could come in. He closed the door and readied himself for the blow he imagined was about to come.

"She's been kidnapped." Frank's pale blue eyes were red-rimmed, his face ashen. "We just had a call from her parents, telling us they'd heard from the kidnappers in the middle of the night." He paused, and Ramon saw the man's Adam's apple slide up and then down again. "They . . . they want a million dollars. And they have three days to figure out where to get it."

Ramon felt his eyes widen. A million dollars! He imagined Julia had a nice home in the States and lived a relatively comfortable life. But a million dollars? Who had that kind of money?

He backed into the rocking chair nearest the front door and nearly collapsed into it. "A million dollars?" He stared up at Frank, connecting with the man's hopeless expression. "In three days? Impossible." He shook his head and buried it in his hands. "It is a death sentence."

He heard Frank pull up another chair and sit down beside him. "That was my first reaction too. Carolyn and I have been talking about this and praying since the Lawsons called us a couple hours ago. It's still hard to believe. We know these things happen in the cities all the time, but not here. True, the locals don't welcome us, and we're well aware of the dangers of living here, which is why we warned Julia not to go out alone. But kidnapping for ransom? I've never heard of it happening here, have you?"

Ramon groaned and shook his head. It made no sense. He didn't want it to be true, and yet he sensed it was.

Frank laid a hand on Ramon's arm. "As unbelievable and hopeless as it sounds, we have to remember there is nothing impossible with God. We need a miracle, Padre. We must gather together for prayer." He squeezed Ramon's arm. "It's our only hope."

Ramon raised his head. He knew his friend was right. None of them had any possible way of gathering together anything close to a million dollars, particularly not in three days. And though he knew nothing of Julia's financial means or that of her family, he couldn't imagine how they could do so either.

Frank was right. They needed a miracle. And though they couldn't produce one, they served a God who spoke creation into existence.

He nodded. "Yes, I will come to your home right away."

"We'll be waiting for you," Frank said, then rose and walked out the door.

★ ★ ★

HERNANDO COULDN'T WAIT for the morning to come to an end. El Toro had announced he was leaving by noontime, so at last he would be able to implement his plan to enjoy his captive to the fullest. Until then he was biding his time, though pleased that he had managed to gain the needed information so easily and to contact her family.

You have no idea how much I am going to enjoy the next few days with you, Señora Julia—and how much you will despise them. But you have no choice, do you? Once El Toro leaves, I am in charge. It is obvious that you are not a courageous woman, so you will do whatever I say. And perhaps, if your family delivers the money, you will go free. Then again, I may decide it is too dangerous to turn you loose so long as I am still living here. We will just have to see what happens, won't we?

He sat on an old stool beside the door to the shed where his captive remained tied to a chair. He had spent the night there, sleeping on the old mattress, and checking on her periodically. Occasionally he saw that she had dozed off, but most of the time he heard her across the room moaning or crying—even praying a time or two.

With the sun almost directly overhead, he smirked. *Praying. Ha! Does she think some imaginary God is going to come on a white horse and rescue her? She is mine now, and soon she will understand that she goes or stays, even lives and breathes, at my command. I have been her god from the moment I caught her in the forest, and I alone will decide her fate.*

The back door to the house opened then, and El Toro stepped outside, followed by his two henchmen. Without thinking, Hernando smiled. They were leaving now—at last.

Hernando rose from his perch and stepped toward the three men, more than ready to bid them farewell.

"So you are leaving now," he said.

El Toro squinted down at him. "You are glad of that, no?"

Hernando lifted his eyebrows. "Not really, no. I just meant—"

"I know what you meant. Once I am gone you will be able to do what you want." El Toro's jaw twitched, and he lifted a meaty finger directly in front of Hernando's face. "I think you forget your mission here. It is not to enjoy yourself with the woman, but to make sure you get the money for El Jefe."

Hernando felt his eyes go wide and his cheeks flame. "I have not forgotten. Not at all. That is why I worked so hard to find this Americana and bring her here. I have already contacted her *familia*, you know that."

El Toro nodded. "Sí. I know that. I also know you look at the woman with lust." He shrugged. "It is no matter to me what you do with her—rape her, beat her, kill her if you must. But not until you have retrieved the money and sent it to El Jefe. Comprende?"

Hernando swallowed the retort that had nearly burst forth from his lips. Raul and the others had joined them outside and were watching him. Hernando knew that keeping cool was the key here. Just play along and get rid of the man; he could do what he wanted once El Toro was gone.

"I understand," he answered, keeping his voice steady. "I would not dream of jeopardizing this payoff."

"See that you don't," El Toro warned. Then he turned and took in the entire group with one dark look. "But just in case you forget, I am going to leave these instructions for all of you." He returned his attention to Hernando. "Until that money is in El Jefe's hands, I don't want any of you alone with that woman—never. Not for a moment. At least two of you are to be with her at all times, day or night." He leaned down slightly, nearly touching Hernando's face. "You will *all* pay the price if I find out you disobeyed—and I will find out. But you, amigo, will pay it first. Comprende?"

Hernando had seen more than once what El Toro could do to someone who crossed him. It wasn't pretty, and it wasn't something he wanted to experience personally. He nodded, forbidding himself to tremble. "Sí, El Toro. I understand."

The big man nodded and straightened up. "Bueno." Without another word, he walked to his car, where one of his companions already stood beside the open back door and the other started up the engine.

★ ★ ★

ABUELA HAD BEEN ESPECIALLY QUIET ALL MORNING, and Itzel wondered when they would finally talk about what she had seen the day before. Even after her abuela had gone back to bed and ordered Itzel to go to sleep, it had been hours before the girl finally drifted off. Her eyes were heavy this morning, but her heart was heavier.

Her breakfast of boiled vegetables had stuck in her throat, and now she forced herself to complete her chores of feeding the chickens and gathering eggs. Her abuela had let her sleep longer than usual, and she imagined the birds were annoyed with her, as they clucked louder and flew at her more often.

But at last she was done, and she returned to the house to see if her abuela was ready to talk. The old woman sat at the rough table where they shared their meals, her hands folded in front of her and a serious look on her face. Itzel sat down across from her and waited.

"You must tell me the truth," Abuela said at last, her dark eyes boring into her only grandchild. "Was it all just a bad dream, or did you really see a mean man taking your teacher away in his car?"

Itzel swallowed, clutching and reclutching her hands in her lap. It was important that she convince her abuela that her story was true. And more and more, Itzel was convinced it was. She knew without a doubt that she had seen the mean man's car go by and that she had seen the face of a woman with red curls through the back window. Much of that face had been covered with a blindfold and gag, but one eye had been partially visible. In that eye, Itzel recognized two things: her teacher's identity and her fear.

"It was not a dream," she said, desperately trying to convey her sincerity with her eyes. "I saw it. My teacher was in the back, and she was scared."

Abuela watched her in silence for a moment and then asked, "What did the car look like?"

"It was . . . different. Not a car, really, and not a truck."

Abuela frowned, and Itzel tried to explain. "It was bigger than a car, but not open in the back like a truck."

Itzel waited until she saw a light of understanding in her grandmother's eyes. The old woman nodded, and Itzel continued.

"It was white—and dirty. It had dents and rust. I saw it the day before when we were at the marketplace. The man who drives it said bad words, and he looked very mean. That's why I remember him."

The old woman nodded again, and Itzel noticed that she had an odd expression on her face.

★ CHAPTER 24 ★

JULIA WAS TERRIFIED. The last thing the man named Hernando had said to her was, "It won't be long now, cara. Soon your protector will be gone, and I will have you all to myself." She had no idea who her protector was supposed to be, but whoever he was, she wished he'd stick around.

On the plus side, when Hernando walked outside the room where she was being held prisoner, he took the dog with him. She'd heard him call the dog Bruno, and though she had yet to see the beast, she'd heard him bark and growl. It was obvious he was no fuzzy little ankle biter.

What is going to happen to me, God? she asked, probably for the hundredth time. *I need You to help me. There is no one else.* And yet the silence continued.

She shifted in the hard seat, trying to get comfortable, but it was no use. She'd been here for hours and had been out of the chair only once. The shame of that memory made her cheeks flame. To think that this horrible man had stripped her and then watched her clean herself was enough to bring on another round of tears, though she fought them with what little strength she had. She'd already nearly choked while sobbing into her gag, and the fear that she might actually suffocate if she gave full vent to her grief enabled her to stop weeping.

Breathing slowly through her nose, she leaned back against the chair, her bound muscles screaming for relief. Never in her life had she experienced such a complete and utter sense of hopelessness. She had made a stupid mistake, a dangerous choice, and now she would no doubt pay for it with her life. Worse yet was the knowledge of what this would do to her aging parents and vulnerable children. What she wouldn't give to be home with them now at this very moment! But deep inside she doubted she would ever see them again.

She heard the door open then, and the man named Hernando greeted her.

"Hello, Señora Julia. How is my preciosa today? Are you hungry? I will bring you something to eat soon, but first you must need to relieve yourself, no?" He approached her then and leaned down to speak into her ear. "Unless you have already soiled yourself again and you wish me to clean you this time."

Julia jerked her head away as Hernando laughed. She desperately needed to use the restroom, but she had determined to hold it as long as necessary.

She heard Bruno growl as Hernando untied her, and she was careful not to make any sudden moves. At last Hernando lifted her to her feet, but her knees nearly buckled beneath her.

"Ah, I see the señora needs me to hold her up." He slid an arm around her waist. "I am happy to help, cara. Now come. You can lean on me."

Another voice interrupted her thoughts then, one of the male voices she'd heard earlier. "Do you need my help, Hernando?"

"No. I can handle this by myself."

So she and Hernando were not alone. Who was the other man? The protector Hernando had mentioned? She certainly hoped so.

As much as she hated to do it, she leaned on Hernando then as she shuffled a few steps ahead. Then he stopped and turned her around. "Let me have your blanket," he said. "Then I will guide you as you sit down."

Horrified, Julia realized there was no separate bathroom. The best she could hope for was that she would be sitting down on an actual toilet.

Reluctantly she removed the blanket and held it out to him, humiliated to think she was stark naked and had to relieve herself in front of two men and a dog. With an audible smirk Hernando took the blanket, put it somewhere, and then placed both hands on her bare arms as he lowered her to the cold rim, which seemed to be nothing more than the edges of a large bucket.

"Sorry there is no privacy, señora, but we are not accustomed to having such a fine visitor in our humble little shed." He laughed then, as did the other man, and once again Julia blinked back tears.

At last they were through with this part of her ordeal, and Hernando walked her back to her chair. This time, though, he dressed her in a shirt and a pair of pants that reeked of sweat and were far too large for her. But she didn't care. She had fully expected one or both of the men to rape her while she was naked and vulnerable. Instead Hernando had dressed her and was now tying her up once again. It was the first time she had realized how really grateful she could be for something that would otherwise seem like a curse. But at the moment, being dressed in smelly old clothes and tied to a chair was quite a bit better than what she had anticipated.

She breathed a sigh of relief. *Thank You, Lord,* she prayed silently, surprised at her gratitude in the midst of such danger.

★ ★ ★

HERNANDO WAS FURIOUS, but he wasn't about to let anyone else see it. As he and Raul went to the house to get some food for the woman, he fumed silently at the unfairness of it all. Hadn't he found the woman on his own? Hadn't he been the one to grab her and bring her there and get her family's contact information? And now he was being told he could not spend time alone with her. And there was no doubt that his compadres wouldn't cross El Toro and allow Hernando to follow through with his plans for the señora.

At least not now, he thought, warming a tortilla before filling it with beans. *But once that money is delivered, she's mine. Nobody touches her but me.*

The thought occurred to him then that the money might very well not come through, but all that meant was that the woman had to be disposed of—one way or the other. And he would certainly take full advantage of the situation before that happened.

With a plate full of three large burritos, he made his way back to the shed, with Raul following close behind carrying a couple of *cervezas.* There was nothing like a cold beer to wash down a warm burrito, he thought, though he doubted he could get the woman to share his drink with him.

I will try, though. El Toro didn't say I couldn't have a little fun with her while we wait. He just said I couldn't be alone with her, and I'm sure not going to take her while Raul or one of the others is there. They'll just want in on the action. So for now, I will toy with her but nothing more. And I will make sure no one else tries anything either. She's mine. I will wait for now, but I will not share her.

He opened the shed door and went inside, with Raul following close behind. Bruno sniffed the air and quickly came to Hernando's side, whining.

"I will share my burrito with you, *perro,* but I will share nothing else—with you or anyone."

★ ★ ★

"**PASTOR MARTIN IS ON HIS WAY OVER,**" John said as he hung up the phone, eyeing his wife with concern. She'd seemed on the edge of a meltdown since their late-night call. "Several others are coming too."

Marie nodded. "That's good," she said, her voice hushed. "I'll make coffee. I still have leftover pie from Thanksgiving. I'll set that out."

John went to her and wrapped his arms around her, pulling her close. "They aren't coming here to eat, sweetheart. They're coming to pray. And they're all powerful prayer warriors, you know that." He kissed the top of her head. "God will hear us, Marie. He knows where Julia is, and He can keep her safe."

"But the million dollars," Marie protested without looking up. "So much money! John, we can't possibly come up with it."

John's heart squeezed. "I know," he said. "And God knows that too. I don't have any easy answers for you, honey, but I can promise you that Julia is safe in our Father's hands."

Marie lifted her head then, and her gray eyes brimmed with tears. "Being safe with the Father could mean He takes her home." She shook her head. "I couldn't bear that, John. I just couldn't."

John swallowed a sob. He had to stay strong. "God will take care of Julia, and He will take care of us too—whatever happens. We have to trust Him, Marie. We have to." He shook his head, and his voice cracked. "What other choice do we have?"

He saw the doubt in her eyes, and then she broke away. "I'm going to go make that coffee now. And I'm setting the pie out, whether they want it or not. I need to do something. And besides, even if they don't eat it, Tyler or Brittney might."

John sighed. He'd been through some hard times in his life, but this was the toughest thing he'd been up against, ever. It would be slightly easier if his grandchildren were dedicated believers, but then their father hadn't been and their mother really wasn't either, so what could he expect? He did hope this situation would help bring them all around, though. And hadn't he seen a little turn in Brittney's attitude lately?

His thoughts returned to Julia then. His father's heart cried out to rescue her, but it was impossible. He could only pray that God would be merciful and rescue her, though the circumstances seemed impossible. "There is nothing too hard for You, Lord," he whispered. "Nothing. You could send an angel to rescue her if that was Your purpose. But I know, ultimately, Your desire—and mine—is to see Julia turn back to You with all her heart. And if that's all that comes out of this, I will praise You for it, Father." His voice broke again. "But oh, Lord, please, rescue my baby! Bring her home to us safe, please, Father!"

The doorbell rang then, and John took a deep breath and squared his shoulders. This was no time to fall apart. He must join together with his wife and pastor and friends to pray for the rescue and return of his daughter. More than that, he must find the strength to release his precious Julia into God's hands—whatever happened. But finding the strength for such a full surrender could never come from his own resources. He needed the support of other believers to help him get to that place of grabbing hold of God's strength and mercy, and then hanging on by his fingernails to the very end.

★ CHAPTER 25 ★

THE OLD WOMAN'S FEET felt like lead as she trudged toward the compound that Saturday afternoon, Itzel at her side. The last thing she wanted was to go and talk to these people she did not know or understand, even though they helped Itzel learn about the marks inside of the books she brought home. But she had come to believe that her grand-daughter might be telling the truth, particularly since she'd checked around with those who knew such things and had the girl's story confirmed. She'd even received additional information that the man's vehicle was something called a Blazer and that he was from San Cristobal. If any of this was true, she needed to let the people at the compound know, whether she wanted to go there or not. If she found out it was not true, she would ignore her sources and deal with Itzel when they got home.

Abuela frowned when they arrived at the compound and found the gate closed and locked. Usually it stood open when she came to bring Itzel to school or to pick her up. How were they to get in?

Itzel pointed to a large bell that hung from the fence beside the gate, and the old woman nodded. She yanked it and then pulled back at the loud jangle that resounded.

Within minutes the gate was cracked open, and a man the old woman recognized as Señor Barnes peered out. When his pale-blue eyes registered recognition, he nodded and pulled the gate open, motioning them inside.

"Greetings, señora . . . and Itzel," he said, his voice subdued and his smile more forced than usual. Abuela began to suspect that something truly was wrong here and her news might be important after all.

"How are you, señora?" Señor Barnes asked, his brows drawing together in a frown. "Though I am pleased to see you, as always, I am surprised that you came today because there is no school. Is something wrong?"

The old woman wished yet again that she could be anywhere other than where she was at this moment, but she sensed it was important that she tell this man what she'd heard from Itzel and the others. She nodded. "Sí," she answered, her voice so low that he stepped closer to hear. "I believe I have news for you about Itzel's teacher."

The man's eyes grew wide. After a moment he nodded and invited them to come to his home. Reluctantly the old woman followed. As many times as she'd come to La Paz because of Itzel's school, she had never gone inside any of the buildings and was not comfortable doing so now. But she pressed her lips together, took Itzel by the hand, and stepped into the man's house.

The size of it was even bigger than she'd expected. She imagined there must be at least three rooms, but it was difficult for her to visualize. Instead she focused on Señora Barnes, who met them at the door and escorted them to the kitchen, where they all sat down around a square wooden table.

"Would you like some tea?" the woman asked.

Abuela was about to decline when she realized it would be rude. As anxious as she was to get out of there, she must now sit long enough to drink one cup of the hot, herbal liquid.

She nodded her thanks and waited until the four of them were all seated around the table, steaming cups in front of them. She wished someone would start the conversation. At last Señor Barnes did so.

"Señora, you said you have news about Julia Bennington."

The old woman frowned. She was not aware of the teacher's name, nor did she care to know, but it wasn't important. All that mattered was to deliver her news, true or not, drink her tea, and get out of there.

She raised her head and found both Señor and Señora Barnes studying her, no doubt waiting for her to tell them what she knew. "Yesterday, at the marketplace, Itzel saw . . . something." She flicked a gaze at her granddaughter, who sat silently, head bowed, beside her. "She said it was a big, white car—or truck—driving by. There was a woman with red hair in the back of the truck, trying to look out the window."

Señor Barnes laid his hand over his wife's, as they both leaned forward. "Trying to look out?" Señor Barnes asked. "What do you mean?"

Abuela glanced again at Itzel, who hadn't moved. Then she continued. "Itzel says she had something over her eyes so she couldn't see, but one eye peeked out underneath. She . . . also had something in her mouth so she couldn't speak."

She heard Señora Barnes gasp and saw her husband squeeze her hand.

The man tore his gaze from Abuela and transferred it to the girl. "Itzel," he asked, his voice firm but gentle, "are you sure it was Señora Bennington?"

For the first time since entering the compound, the child lifted her gaze. Abuela spotted tears on her cheeks. Itzel nodded. "Sí. It was my teacher."

The silence lasted only a moment before the old woman continued. "I have heard it from others too. It is said the car is called a Blazer, and the man who drives it might be from San Cristobal, but he has not been around here long." She swallowed, the length of her sentence exhausting her. She lifted her teacup and sipped from it, more anxious than ever to leave.

She watched as the two who sat across from her looked at one another, then back at her. "I can't thank you enough, señora. Your news is exactly what we needed to hear." He smiled, but Abuela could tell it was forced. "Is there . . . anything else?"

She shook her head. "That is all I have heard. I came right away to tell you."

Señor Barnes nodded. "And we are grateful that you did. Thank you. If you hear anything else, please tell us, will you?"

"Sí." Taking a final drink of tea, the old woman stood to her feet and nudged Itzel's shoulder to do the same.

The child obeyed, but before turning to leave, she fixed her eyes on the Barneses. "Is my . . . teacher OK?"

Once again the Barneses exchanged glances before the woman smiled at the girl. "We must pray that she is, Itzel. Will you pray as well?"

The girl nodded and then dropped her head once again as Señor Barnes headed for the door. Abuela took her granddaughter's hand and followed him outside.

★ ★ ★

ITZEL WAS RELIEVED when they arrived back at home. One of her friends had called out to her as they passed by, inviting her to come and play. But Itzel ignored her, continuing her silent trudge home. All she wanted was to lie down on her sleeping mat and be alone.

As sure as she'd been that the red-haired woman she'd seen peering out the back window of the white car was her teacher, she had clung to a tiny hope that she was wrong, that her teacher would greet her at the compound when they arrived. But that hadn't happened. Instead, after talking with Señor and Señora Barnes, Itzel had known with even greater certainty that her beloved teacher was in great danger.

The little girl lay down on her mat and drew her knees up to her chest. Even when her abuela offered to take her to the marketplace for a special treat, she refused to move. She was not interested in going anywhere or eating anything. She had promised to pray for Señora Bennington, and though she wasn't sure how to do that, she would try—and she wouldn't stop until she heard her teacher was safe.

★ ★ ★

JOHN AND MARIE LAY SILENTLY, side by side, in their bed that night. The prayer meeting had lasted for several hours, and Marie was encouraged by the time everyone left. It hadn't taken long, however, to sink back into despair, though she'd held it together long enough to prepare a quick supper. None of them had seemed inclined to eat much, but it had helped Marie to do something familiar. Afterward she and Brittney had cleaned up while John and Tyler once again watched television. At last they all gave up and headed upstairs to bed.

Marie imagined no one had drifted off to sleep yet, but maybe it was best that they were alone with their thoughts—and prayers. *Why is it my faith rises to the surface when others are here, praying with us, and then it bottoms out when they leave? I am so weak, Lord. So weak!*

She choked back a sob, not wanting to disturb her husband. But almost instantly he stretched out his arm and drew her to him. She laid her head on his chest, grateful for his closeness.

"What's going to happen?" she whispered. "What will they do to her when the three days pass and we don't have the million dollars to give them? What will they do to her, John?"

She felt her husband shudder. "I don't know, sweetheart. But we can't focus on that. We have to stay focused on God, who not only knows where Julia is but what lies ahead for all of us." He bent to kiss the top of her head. "Remember, He loves her even more than we do."

Marie knew that in her mind, but her heart still had questions. If God truly loved Julia more than her own parents did, why had He allowed her to be kidnapped in the first place? As an earthly parent, Marie would never have let this happen. It just didn't make sense. Even if Julia came through it safe and sound, what possible good could come of it?

As if reading her thoughts, John stroked her hair and said, "We don't always understand God's thoughts or His ways because they're so far beyond our capacity to do so. But one thing we can be sure of is that His plans for us—and for Julia—are for good and not for evil, to give her a future and a hope, just as the Scriptures promise."

Jeremiah 29:11. One of Marie's favorite verses. She remembered helping Julia learn it when she was a child and needed to recite it for Sunday School. The thought occurred to her that it might encourage Julia right now, wherever she was and whatever was happening to her.

"Please," she said, raising her head to look into her husband's eyes, "pray with me that God will remind Julia of that verse. She knows it. She memorized it years ago. I think she needs to be reminded of it right now."

John nodded and held his wife close as he implored the Lord to bring that verse to their daughter's mind and to encourage her to cling to it, no matter what.

★ CHAPTER 26 ★

JULIA SLEPT INTERMITTENTLY but had no idea whether it was day or night. Every few hours, though not nearly often enough, Hernando untied her so she could avail herself of the primitive facilities. And though she heard other men's voices now and then, always Hernando seemed to be there. It was obvious he felt territorial about her, but for whatever reason he had yet to carry out his threat to rape her. For that she was indeed grateful.

He had recently brought her another burrito, which seemed to be the only fare she was allowed—or perhaps all they had. Either way, she was grateful for that as well. She had originally thought she would never be able to eat anything, but despite her painful and frightening circumstances, her stomach still seemed to growl its demand for food.

Now she listened to the intermittent snores of at least two men. Did that mean it was night? She occasionally heard what sounded like a dog whimpering in sleep, so perhaps it was. But which night? How many nights had she been here? Hernando had told her that her family had three days to pay her ransom—one million dollars—so she could only assume the three days hadn't come and gone yet or they would most certainly have killed her by now.

She shifted in her chair once again, desperately trying to find a more comfortable position. Sleep was nearly impossible, but at least Hernando wasn't taunting her at the moment—another point of gratitude.

I know the plans I have for you . . .

The words took shape in her mind, unbidden and yet somehow welcome. She frowned. Jeremiah 29:11. She hadn't thought of that verse in years, but she remembered well the many evenings she sat with her mother, memorizing Scripture verses so she could recite them in Sunday School. She'd had a perfect attendance record then and more gold stars for Scripture memorization than almost anyone else in her class. When and how had she drifted so far from the faith of her childhood?

Tom. My beloved Tom. Handsome, sweet, thoughtful man that you were. You rode into my life like a knight in shining armor and swept me off my feet, as they say. You became the most important thing in my life, more so even than God. Is that what happened to my faith? Did I allow it to be replaced with love for you?

She sighed. No doubt that was at least part of the reason, but she couldn't blame Tom for that. Though he had no personal faith of his own, he'd never insisted she leave hers behind.

But I did, didn't I, Lord? Slowly but surely, I let it slip down my priority list until it nearly vanished altogether. When Mom and Dad's pastor came out to pray with Tom before he died, I was so pleased that he received Jesus as his Savior, even if it was in the last days of his life. But even then, I continued to drift along on my own way instead of Yours, God. It just seemed so much easier at the time.

A sob escaped her throat then. *And look at where I ended up. Is this to be the end of my life, Lord? I've ignored You for so long, and I know I don't have a right to ask, but Father, please . . . I can't even imagine what this will do to my family, what will become of them if I die here in this awful place.*

The remembered promise came back to her again, this time in more detail. *I know the plans I have for you, plans for good and not for evil, to give you a future and a hope.*

Another sob burst forth then, and she didn't even try to hold back the tears. Was God saying He wasn't through with her yet, that there was still hope for her? Did she dare cling to such a fragile thread?

"Shut up over there," came a growled order. "We're trying to sleep."

Julia knew it wasn't Hernando's voice, but one of the others. She tried to obey, tried to turn off the water works, but the tears continued to come, once again soaking the filthy rag that covered her eyes. Worse than that was the gag that threatened to suffocate her if she didn't stop crying. For that reason even more than her captor's order, she tried yet again to calm herself. She had nearly succeeded in doing so when she felt, as well as heard, Hernando's voice beside her ear.

"What is it, cara? Are you lonely? Do you miss Hernando?" He laughed. "Yes, I think that must be it." He kissed the top of her ear. "Do not worry, preciosa. As soon as your familia sends the money, then we can have our time together—alone. Just you and me, señora." He laughed again. "But you are impatient, no? Tired of waiting? Maybe a little kiss from Hernando will make you feel better."

She felt him untie the gag, the only time he had done so except when he gave her food. But even the relief of having her mouth free didn't calm the terror or revulsion that rose up inside her as he brought his lips close to hers, his foul breath assaulting her. The promised words from the Scriptures that had so recently brought her comfort now evaporated as she tried to pull back from him. The back of the chair prevented that, and as his mouth closed over hers she bit down on his lower lip until he screamed. When she still refused to let go, he slapped her so hard her mouth flew open in a scream of her own.

By now Bruno was awake and growling, and Hernando was free. But before she could catch her breath, he grabbed her by the hair, yanking her head back as he spit in her face. "If you ever try that again, señora," he hissed, "I will repay you—slowly and painfully—until you beg me to kill you." He yanked her hair again, and Julia knew he had pulled some of it out. Tears once again streamed from her eyes as she tried to respond, but he held her head so tightly she couldn't nod.

"I . . . understand," she managed to say at last.

"Good." He loosened his grip slightly. "That is very good, señora. Do not forget it. You belong to me now. Comprende?"

This time she was able to nod, though only slightly. She waited, hoping he would release her then. Instead the other man's voice interrupted them.

"Hey, I told you, I'm trying to get some sleep. If you want to beat the woman, can you wait until morning?"

At last Hernando dropped his grip and moved away from her face. Would he heed his companion's request and at least leave her alone for now?

After several seconds where the only sound she heard was an agitated Bruno, Hernando apparently decided to call it a night and replaced the gag in her mouth. As much as she hated it, she breathed a ragged sigh of relief. Perhaps she would live for at least a few more hours.

RAMON WAS AS CLOSE TO ECSTATIC as he could be under such dire circumstances. True, Julia was still missing and the kidnappers had demanded an impossible amount of money in a ridiculously short period of time. But he knew that kidnappers often demanded ransoms beyond the actual amount they would accept. He could only hope that was the case this time. But his real reason for optimism—as fragile as it might be—was the news that Itzel's abuela had brought them. He still had little or no hope that local authorities, either in Chamula or in San Cristobal, would do anything to help them, but at least he had a starting place.

He wished he could head out to San Cristobal immediately, but it was Sunday morning and he needed to keep his priorities straight. First things first. He would lead the church service, as well as more prayer for Julia's rescue, and then he and Frank Barnes would head into San Juan to search for the white Blazer. He knew it would take a miracle to find it in this city of approximately fifty thousand people, but surely God would help them. *All the more reason to wait until after the church service and our prayers,* he reminded himself.

Ramon took his usual place in the front of the chapel, sitting on his stool and holding his guitar. *Help me to focus on worshipping You, Lord,* he prayed silently as he strummed his first chords.

The front gate to the compound was open, and the small congregation was beginning to stream in. Ramon watched as they entered and took their seats. Few of them knew of Julia's kidnapping, and he wrestled with whether or not to announce it and ask for group prayer. But even before they joined him in the first song, he sensed a peace from God that he should indeed invite them to pray together. With that settled, he continued the worship service with a stronger assurance.

★ ★ ★

MARIE WONDERED IF she'd lost her mind when she agreed to join Ginny after church to help serve lunch at the homeless shelter. Yet the moment Ginny had invited her, she felt compelled to go.

John had seemed mildly surprised but then encouraged her to take advantage of this ministry opportunity, assuring her he would go home and pick up Brittney and Tyler and take them out for lunch. "It will help you get your mind off Julia for a little while, and it might do the kids good to get away from the house. You know how tough it's going to be to convince them to go back to school this evening anyway, but I really think they should. Maybe I can lay some groundwork for that while we're at the restaurant."

Marie knew he was right that it would be best for their grandchildren to return to school, but she didn't tell him she'd much prefer it if they stayed. Deep down she imagined that's exactly what they would end up doing, no matter how much groundwork John managed to lay. Besides, she and John were heading to their bank first thing Monday morning to see how much money they could pull together to at least attempt a ransom payment. Tyler and Brittney knew about the planned trip to the bank and would no doubt want to stick around to see how it turned out.

Ginny knew about the situation with Julia, which was a comfort to Marie. As they parked in the street in front of the shelter, Marie was shocked to see the length of the line of people waiting to be fed.

Nothing can take away the pain or fear of knowing my daughter is in danger, but maybe I can do some good for someone else while I wait. Marie followed Ginny inside, catching the eyes of hungry men, women, and children as they bypassed the line.

"Hey, the cavalry has arrived!"

Marie looked up to see Joe Littleton, the main chef at the shelter, his face beaming in welcome as he stood in the kitchen door. A handful of volunteers already worked at covering long tables with white paper, distributing salt and pepper shakers, and placing plastic bowls of sugar and powdered creamer packets on each table. From the looks of the many people waiting to be fed, it would take a concerted effort from everyone inside to pull this off in a timely manner.

"I think we've got enough people out here getting the tables ready," Joe said, his ample stomach covered by an oversized apron that said, *Time to Eat!* He gestured to Ginny and Marie. "I need a couple of extra hands to finish making salad and dishing it into plastic bowls. Think you two can handle that?"

"Absolutely," Ginny said, laughing as she led the way. Marie was right behind her, and in moments they were wearing aprons identical to Joe's. Three other people stirred soup and buttered bread, while one young woman sliced several sheet cakes and placed the pieces on small paper plates.

It was a busy half hour or so, but before Marie knew it, the line was moving past as she and the others placed helpings of food on each tray. A few of those in line met her eyes, but most looked down at their trays. Some said thank you; some asked for more; others were silent.

At last they all were fed, and Ginny encouraged Marie to join her in walking around the room and greeting the diners, stopping to visit only if someone seemed open. Hesitantly, Marie did so. It was the first time she had actually intermingled with the homeless they served.

She received a few mumbled words from the first couple of people she talked to, but then an elderly woman with scraggly white hair looked up from her meal and offered a toothless smile. "I'm Gladys. Who are you?"

Marie lifted her eyebrows. This one looked promising. Maybe she'd sit down and talk with her for a few minutes before moving on. She took the empty seat beside the woman named Gladys.

"I'm Marie," she said, smiling in return. "It's nice to meet you, Gladys."

The woman nodded and took a bite of chocolate cake. "I love cake," she said and then began to hum as she chewed.

Marie recognized the tune. "Amazing Grace," she said. "One of my favorite hymns."

"Mine too," the woman said, washing down her cake with a sip of coffee. "God wrote it for me, you know."

Marie lifted her eyebrows. "He did?"

Gladys nodded. "He sure did." She leaned toward her, the dirty lapel of her jacket touching the frosting on her cake. "Especially the part about being lost before He found me." She laughed. "He knew where I was all the time. It was just me that didn't know where I was." She pointed her fork at Marie. "But I know now. Yes, ma'am, I know exactly where I am. I'm on my way home." She nodded sharply. "And I'm gonna make it too. You know why?"

The woman paused, and Marie realized she was waiting for a reply. "Um . . . no, why?"

Gladys looked surprised. "Because it's up to Him to get me there. Didn't you know that?" She frowned and shook her head. "Only God can get us home safe, you know."

A vision of Julia popped into Marie's mind, and for a brief moment she chastised herself for having forgotten about her daughter's situation. And then she focused on Gladys once again. What had she said? *Only God can get us home safe.* Oh, how true that was, and how desperately she needed to hang on to that great truth right now! And to think she'd been reminded of it by a woman who had no earthly home of her own.

Thank You, Lord, she prayed silently. Out loud she said, "Thank you for that, Gladys. God has used you to encourage me today."

Gladys beamed and went back to eating her cake and humming.

★ CHAPTER 27 ★

It seemed that Frank and Ramon had driven Frank's old Jeep up and down every residential street in San Cristobal, though Ramon knew that wasn't even close to the case. But they'd been at for hours, with no promising leads.

"We've spotted five Blazers today," Frank commented, his eyes still on the road ahead. "Only one of them was even close to white, and it's up on jacks, so I doubt it's been driven in ages. Even if we come across the right one, how will we know?"

Ramon had wondered the same thing countless times, but each time he had come to the same conclusion. "God would let us know," he said, scanning the dirt yards in one of the older neighborhoods where they'd learned at least some drug usage and gang activity were present.

"They probably wouldn't leave the vehicle outside for anyone to see," Frank said.

Ramon had thought of that too. "God knows," he said. It was the only answer he had.

As the sun eased down to the western horizon, Ramon fought the sense that his heart and his hope were sinking with it. He knew they couldn't stay out searching all night, but they couldn't give up yet.

"You know we're going to have to get back soon."

Frank had such a way of stating the obvious, and yet doing so as gently as possible. It didn't lessen the pain, but at least Ramon knew that Frank felt nearly as badly about giving up the search as he did.

"I know." Ramon sighed. "I was so sure we would find something today."

"In God's time," Frank said.

Ramon cut his eyes toward his companion and nodded. "Sí. In God's time." He took a deep breath. "One more hour?"

"Sure. One more hour. Then we head back." Frank extended a hand to his friend's shoulder. "That doesn't mean we're giving up. We can come back, you know."

The three-day limit until Julia's exorbitant ransom was due loomed in Ramon's thoughts. If they didn't find her tonight, they would have only one day left.

★ ★ ★

A COLD FOG HAD MOVED IN OVERNIGHT, and though Julia couldn't see it, her teeth chattered as she shivered on the chair, trying not to give up all hope. The memory of her white shawl, tucked inside the shopping bag she'd dropped on the jungle floor, teased her with thoughts of soft warmth and comfort. Would she ever be comfortable again? How much longer could she survive tied to a chair, being given food and water in smaller doses now and receiving much rougher treatment from her captors?

She knew she had made a terrible mistake when she bit Hernando's lip. He had been furious with her ever since, slapping her more than once and screaming at her to shut up each time she broke down and cried. But what else could she have done? The thought of that filthy, evil man kissing her had all but caused her to vomit. She tried not to think of how much worse it would be if he carried out his threats to rape her, though he hadn't used that term.

It's what he means. He says things like, "We will have fun together" and "We will finally be able to be alone, away from the others." It was an image she simply could not allow herself to picture in her mind. She would rather be dead. Yes, she had come to that conclusion. Death would be preferable to yielding her body to such a vile man who no doubt would kill her when he was through anyway.

I might still have a chance if there were any way at all that my family could somehow get the ransom. But a million dollars? They couldn't come up with a fraction of that, at least not on such short notice.

Three days. Has it been that long yet? Am I almost out of time?

Tears threatened again, but she refused to let them come. Hernando and one of his companions were snoring, and she didn't want to risk another angry confrontation. At least while they slept, the icy room was relatively peaceful. She wished she too could drift off to sleep and forget about her plight . . . at least for a little while.

I know the plans I have for you . . .

The words washed over her like warm honey, reviving the tiny spark of hope that still lingered in her otherwise broken heart.

★ ★ ★

HERNANDO WAS FURIOUS. He woke up angry on Monday morning, and he grew angrier as the day progressed. He would never forgive that woman for hurting him the way she did. Who did she think she was? She would learn soon enough, regardless of how things went today regarding the ransom.

It was cold this morning, with the mist not burning off as it usually did after the sun rose. He slipped on a jacket as he went outside to make the call on his disposable cellular phone. It was important that his calls were untraceable, and he also wanted privacy while he connected with the woman's family. He was glad they had fairly reliable phone service here in San Cristobal, at least most of the time.

He dialed and was pleased that the call went through on the first try. A man answered this time, and it was obvious he was trying to seem calm and confident, but Hernando knew he had to be shaking inside.

"Do you have the money?" Hernando demanded.

After a slight pause, the man answered. "We will have . . . some of it . . . in a couple of hours. We're about to go to the bank to pick it up."

Exactly what Hernando had expected . . . but not acceptable. He added a threatening tone to his voice. "I told you a million dollars—all of it, not some of it. The señora is your daughter, no?"

Another pause. This time the man's words betrayed his anxiety. "Yes. Please don't hurt her."

Hernando laughed. "Oh, I've already hurt her, and I will hurt her a lot more now that I know you don't care enough to send the money for her freedom."

"No!" The man was nearly crying now. "No, please, I'm trying to get as much as possible. But . . . a million dollars. It's too much. We aren't rich people."

"You have a home."

"Yes. And we can borrow money against it, but not a million dollars. And it takes time—"

Hernando interrupted him. "You are out of time, señor. I told you, three days."

"Please," the man sobbed. "Please, we'll give you what we have now and get more . . ."

"And how much do you have to send me now?"

The man's voice dropped, and Hernando had to strain to hear him. "I don't know yet, but . . . at least twenty thousand, maybe more if the bank will loan it to me."

"Twenty thousand!" Hernando exploded. "Twenty thousand dollars? That's all your daughter's life is worth to you?"

"No! No, she is worth everything. But . . . we just don't have any more . . . not yet. But we can get more. We just need more time."

"More time for what? To bring in the authorities? You know what will happen if you do that. I told you, remember? Do you want your daughter's head returned to you in a box?"

The man was weeping now. "No. Oh, please, no. Don't kill her. We will send you more as soon as we can, and we won't notify the authorities. I promise!"

"How much?" Hernando demanded. "And how soon can you get it to me?"

"Fifty thousand. Maybe more." He heard the man take a ragged breath. "We could have it in a week, maybe less."

Hernando laughed. "I ask for a million, and you offer me fifty thousand? This is a joke—an insult. Do you really expect me to let her go for fifty thousand dollars?"

"Please," the man begged. "I will get more if I can. I won't know how much until I talk to them at the bank this morning."

Hernando smirked, enjoying the game he played with this man, even though he was angry that he hadn't offered more. "I will give you the instructions to send the twenty thousand now, and then you have one week—one week, no more—to send at least twenty times that much. Do you understand? If I don't have that money one week from today, your daughter will come home to you in pieces. And if you even think about doing something stupid like calling the authorities, you won't even get that much of her back. Comprende?"

Still sobbing, the man managed to agree and take down the instructions. Then, when he begged to speak to his daughter, Hernando ended the call.

"Twenty thousand dollars!" He spit on the ground as he returned to the shed. "From now on I will treat her as the worthless daughter she is. She needs a lesson anyway. I will keep my promise to El Toro for now and not be alone with her, but he never said I couldn't punish her. Now she will see what happens when I am insulted and my patience runs out."

★ CHAPTER 28 ★

JULIA STILL SHIVERED, though more now from fear than from the lingering cold. She'd heard Hernando storm into the building, cursing as he told his companion that her family had come up with only twenty thousand dollars, though they'd offered more if they could have more time.

Despair weighed on her, driving out any shred of hope she might have left. What would happen to her now? Already they treated her worse than when she'd first arrived. It had been hours now since they'd brought her anything to eat, or even given her a sip of water. What else could they possibly do to her? She shuddered as her imagination went into overdrive.

"So what are you going to do?" the other man asked in response to Hernando's tirade. "What will you tell El Toro?"

Hernando cursed again. "I will tell him they sent a down payment, with more to come. If he says to let her live, I will do so. If not, I will happily chop her up into pieces and send her home to her family."

"Do not be hasty, amigo," the man said. "I have heard the curanderos might pay for someone like her."

Julia frowned. She had heard of the curanderos and knew they were somewhat like spiritual gurus to the Mayans—witch doctors, even. But why would they pay a ransom for her?

"You believe they still do those human sacrifice things?" Hernando asked, his tone skeptical.

"Why not? Many of the locals talk about it. What if it's true?"

Human sacrifices? The words rang in Julia's ears, and she felt lightheaded.

Hernando sounded a bit more positive this time. "Maybe you're right. Maybe it wouldn't hurt to find out. Even if we don't get that much from her family, we might be able to sell her after that. All right. It shouldn't be that hard to find some of those curanderos. Put the word out on the street, and let's see if we get a response." He laughed, and she heard him approach.

"Do you hear that, señora?" His mouth was near her ear again. "A human sacrifice. What do you think of that? First we will get as much money from your family as we can. Then I will show you what a real man can do to your body. And finally, we will sell you to a witch doctor and see what they can do to get rid of you once and for all. Then we will see if you regret the way you treated me. I do not forget, cara. You will pay for what you did."

The tears came then, and Julia couldn't stop them. But even as she wept into her blindfold, Hernando jerked the gag from her mouth. "Cry, señora," he hissed. "Weep and wail all you want. I no longer care. In fact, I might very much enjoy listening to you beg. But remember, if you make too much noise you might make Bruno mad. And trust me, preciosa, you do not want to do that. Bruno is not nearly as nice as I am."

He laughed again, even as Bruno growled at the mention of his name. Julia, though grateful to have the gag removed, resolved to cry silently. She didn't want to take any chances of angering Bruno.

★ ★ ★

SCHOOL HAD BEEN CANCELED UNTIL FURTHER NOTICE, and Frank and Padre Ramon sat together at the Barneses' kitchen table on Monday evening, discussing another trip into San Cristobal. Their first two trips there, searching for the white Blazer, had proved fruitless, but Ramon could not let the issue go.

"We have to try again," he insisted. "The kidnappers have called the Lawsons again, and now they know there will be no million dollars. Maybe Señora Bennington's father bought her more time, but maybe he did not. We might be her only hope."

Frank shook his head and buried it in his hands. "I don't know," he groaned. "We found nothing yesterday and nothing today. What makes you think it will be any different tomorrow?" He lifted his head. "I'm beginning to think the Lawsons made a mistake not contacting the authorities in the States. I know the kidnappers threatened to kill Julia if they did, but they may very well do so anyway."

Ramon sighed. "True. But what are the chances the authorities in either country will find her in time? You know the local law enforcement here won't even talk to them or lift a finger to help. I think we have a better chance of finding her ourselves."

Carolyn approached the table then and poured a fresh cup of coffee for each of them. "Are either of you hungry?" she asked.

"Not really," Frank answered.

Ramon shook his head. "No, gracias."

Carolyn nodded, returned the coffee pot to the stove, and left the room.

"Please," Ramon begged, his voice cracking. "One more time. Tomorrow, first thing in the morning."

Frank lifted his head, and their eyes met. At last he nodded. "One more time. In the morning."

★ ★ ★

ITZEL WAS VERY SAD, not only because her teacher was missing but because she could no longer go to school. When her abuela suggested they go to the marketplace that morning and even promised her a special treat, the girl could not get excited.

The mist that had lingered most of the previous day was gone this morning, and even with her heavy heart, Itzel enjoyed the warm sunshine as they walked the short distance to do their shopping. She had spotted her friend as they walked from their home, and once again the girl had invited her to come and play with her later. Her abuela had encouraged her to accept the invitation, but Itzel had declined. She did not feel like playing when her heart was so heavy.

As they made their way through the marketplace, Itzel noticed two of the local curanderas talking together behind one of the stalls. She knew one of them was a friend of her abuela's, so she wasn't surprised when her abuela told her to wait while she went to speak with them.

Itzel obeyed, as she always did, but she watched the lively conversation. She couldn't hear all that was said, but the two women, dressed in their bright colors and wearing their tiny mirrors around their necks to ward off evil spirits, seemed pleased that Itzel's grandmother had joined them.

Finally the conversation came to an end, and Abuela returned. As they finished their shopping and went home, Itzel noticed that her abuela was quieter than usual. She even forgot to get Itzel the treat she had promised. But the girl didn't mention it, as she wasn't especially hungry anyway.

★ CHAPTER 29 ★

THE GATE TO THE COMPOUND WAS OPEN, and Ramon and Frank were in the Jeep and about to head out on Wednesday morning when once again the girl named Itzel and her grandmother showed up. The men climbed out of the vehicle and motioned them to come through the gate. In moments they had ushered them into the Barneses' home, and soon they all sat around the kitchen table. This time the old woman declined Carolyn Barnes's offer of tea.

Knowing the local custom that required courtesy in such a situation, Ramon realized the woman's reason for coming was urgent. He leaned forward, praying silently, as all eyes fell on the old woman.

"There is . . . talk," she said, her eyes downcast as she spoke. Itzel followed suit, keeping her eyes on the table in front of her and her hands folded in her lap.

"What sort of talk, señora?" Frank prodded.

"On the street. Among the curanderas." She lifted her head briefly, her eyes flitting back and forth over the table's other occupants. Then she dropped them again. "They say . . . there is an Americana with . . . red hair. Someone from San Cristobal is trying to sell her for . . ." Her voice trailed off, and Ramon saw her shoulders twitch. "For a sacrifice."

Carolyn Barnes gasped, and her hand flew to her mouth. She turned to her husband, as if waiting for him to say it was impossible. But he didn't. He simply stared at the woman, his eyes wide.

At last Ramon spoke. "Do you think it is true? Would that really happen?"

The old woman shrugged. "I cannot say. Some believe that still happens. The curanderas I talked with, they say they know people . . ."

Once again her voice trailed off, and the only sound Ramon heard was his own heart pounding in his ears. Determined to act on this new information, he said to Frank, "All the more reason we must find her. Now. Today. We cannot wait another minute."

"But how?" Frank said. "How are we going to find her in such a big town? We've driven around some of the neighborhoods already, but there are so many more."

"We will pray," Ramon insisted. "Surely God will lead us to her."

"Frank, Ramon is right," Carolyn insisted, laying her hand on her husband's arm. "We must pray first, and then you have to try to find her. What else can we do?"

Frank shook his head. "I know you're right. I know we have to try. But it seems so impossible. All we know is to look for an old white Blazer. What if it's parked inside a garage somewhere? We'll never find her then."

After another brief silence, the abuela spoke again. "I can help. The curanderas told me the name of the street."

★ ★ ★

BY WEDNESDAY MORNING, Julia's discomfort had turned to agony; her muscles screamed from being tied to the chair for so long. She had no idea how long it had been since they'd fed her, but the hunger didn't bother her nearly as much as the thirst. On the positive side, the men had not replaced the gag after Hernando removed it and told her to go ahead and cry. Though she continued to keep her sobs as silent as possible, she was grateful the gag was finally gone. But she desperately needed to use the bucket to relieve herself.

"Please," she begged, her voice cracking. "Please, help me."

She recognized Hernando's laughter as he bent down to whisper in her ear. "Why should I help you, señora? After what you did to me, you are lucky you are still alive."

She sobbed, trying to reach into her memory for the promise she believed God had given her—something about plans for her, good plans. Where were those good plans? And where was God? Why didn't He help her?

"Por favor," she begged again. "Just some water. Please."

The blow to the side of her head was so strong that the fact she'd been hit scarcely had time to register before everything went black.

★ ★ ★

RAMON AND FRANK covered the distance between Chamula and San Cristobal in record time, and they had gone alone, despite Carolyn's protests.

"It's too dangerous," she'd insisted. "Even if you find the Blazer, what will you do then? You can't just go knock on the door and ask for Julia. At least if I'm with you, I can stay in the Jeep and be ready to help you escape if you need to get away in a hurry."

Ramon knew she was right, but he also knew Frank would never agree to it. He also knew Julia was running out of time, and they were her only hope. He had even offered to go alone, leaving Frank at home with Carolyn. "You two can pray while I'm gone," he'd insisted. "God will direct me, and He will help me. I know it."

But Frank had refused the offer. "No. I can't let you go alone, my friend. I must go with you. But I agree that God will direct us and help us."

When Carolyn began to protest yet again, he lifted his hand to stop her. "I understand how you feel, sweetheart, but I have to go with him. We can't let him go alone, and there is no way we're taking you with us."

"But surely you can find others to go with you," she argued. "Why must it be just the two of you?"

Frank put his hands on her shoulders and gazed down into her eyes. "We have no time to gather others, to explain what we're doing. Ramon is right. Julia is running out of time. But I promise you this. If we get there and locate her and it looks like we can't do anything on our own, we'll at least try to see if the San Cristobal authorities will help us. All right?"

Carolyn hesitated, but at last she nodded, though tears spilled onto her cheeks.

After the three of them prayed together, the men jumped into the Jeep and headed down the road toward San Cristobal, kicking up dust in their wake. And now they had arrived. Frank slowed the vehicle.

"Where to now?"

Ramon, sitting in the passenger seat, looked around. He spotted a small grocery store that looked as if it had been around for a very long time. "Let me run in there and ask. Maybe they'll know where the street is."

He was back within minutes. "They couldn't give me exact directions, but they knew the area of town. It's not far from here." He pointed straight ahead. "That way."

Frank nodded and hit the gas again. Ramon took a deep breath and continued praying, as he'd been doing since they'd driven out of the gates of La Paz.

★ CHAPTER 30 ★

SHE FELT AS IF SHE WERE UNDER WATER, struggling to find her way to the surface so she could breathe again. But the darkness lured her to stay below, to let her last bit of air go so she could float away, far from the pain that engulfed her.

Then she heard the voices. Men—and something else. A dog barking. Where was she? What was going on?

And then, in a terrifying instant, it all came back to her. She wasn't waking up from a nightmare as she'd hoped; she was living it.

The voice she'd come to recognize as belonging to Hernando ordered, "Let the dog out. But keep an eye on him. Call him back when he's through doing his business."

Julia groaned. The pounding in her head was unbearable, but the pressure on her bladder was nearly as bad.

"Are you all right, señora?" The question mocked her as she felt his breath near her ear. "Is there something I can do for you?"

As much as she hated asking, she had no choice. "Bathroom," she whispered. "Please."

Hernando chuckled. "Why, of course, preciosa. I will be happy to help you."

She despised the way the man ran his hands over her body as he untied her and lifted her to her feet, but she was too dizzy to stand on her own so she allowed herself to lean on him as she shuffled, still blindfolded, to the bucket a few steps away. She wished he would at least have the decency to turn away until she was finished, but she knew he wouldn't.

"Are you ready to return to your chair, señora?"

The sarcasm dripped from his words, but she ignored it, answering only with a nod.

"What was that, cara?" He leaned closer. "I did not hear you."

Choking back a sob, she whispered, "Yes . . . please."

Hernando laughed again and nearly shoved her back to the chair. He was about to tie her to it when she heard the door open.

"The other two are going to town to get some supplies. Bruno jumped in the Blazer when the door was open, so he's going with them."

Hernando grunted an acknowledgment before the other man continued.

"I'm going to the house to fix a burrito. Do you want one?"

"Sí. And bring one for the señora." He paused. "No, bring her half a burrito. She is still being punished for what she did to me."

Julia flinched as he grabbed her hair and yanked her head backward. "You will learn to treat me right, señora, do you understand?"

She heard the door close and knew she was alone with her captor. She tried to nod, but he held her head back so fiercely that she could not.

"It won't be long until you are mine to do with as I please," he crooned, his face nearly touching hers. "If your family doesn't come through with a lot more money, we have other options."

Her memory flitted to the conversation she'd overheard about curanderos and human sacrifice. Surely that wasn't a serious possibility!

"And whatever happens to you in the end, I will have you for myself first. Do not forget that, señora."

He nearly spit out the final word as he released his grip on her hair. With it she felt her last shred of hope slip away, even as she felt his lips against her ear yet again. "Since we are alone for a few minutes, maybe I will show you just a little of what you can look forward to, cara."

★ ★ ★

ONCE FRANK AND RAMON found the street it took only a moment to spot the white Blazer. Excitement leapt in Ramon's heart, though he hadn't a clue what to do next.

Pulling to a spot where they could keep an eye on the house and vehicle without being seen themselves, they watched and prayed. Within moments they spotted a man and a dog emerging from the backyard. Frank and Ramon eased down in the seat until they could scarcely peer over the dash.

"What do you think?" Ramon asked.

"I don't know. I just wish we knew how many are in there. If he's the only one, we might have a chance."

Ramon didn't like the looks of the dog, but he thought Frank might be right. Before he could answer, two more men came out of the house and went to the Blazer.

"Now we know he isn't the only one," Ramon said.

Frank nodded as they continued to watch. The men had no sooner opened the vehicle's door than the dog hopped inside. Soon the two men and the dog were headed down the road, leaving the man they'd originally seen behind.

"We still don't know how many others are in there," Ramon said, "but at least those two are gone—and the dog too. What do you think?"

When they saw the man walk inside the house, Frank answered. "We've been praying for the right opportunity, and we know others are praying too. I think it's now or never, amigo."

Their eyes met, and Ramon nodded. He knew Señora Barnes was back at the compound praying. They had also alerted Julia's parents to the latest developments, and they, too, were praying. Frank was right. It was now or never.

He closed his eyes. "Cover us, Father. Go ahead of us, Lord." He opened his eyes. "Let's go."

They climbed out of the Jeep and approached the house. All was quiet. From the corner of his eye, Ramon spotted a shed in the back. Before he could point it out to Frank, a scream pierced the air, and he knew they had located Julia.

★ ★ ★

JULIA'S HEAD THROBBED, and she knew she was completely at Hernando's mercy, despite the fact that he had not yet retied her. She even thought she had given up all hope—until he began to grope her. Instinctively she screamed and raised her hands to rip off her blindfold. She knew she might die before this struggle was over, but she wasn't going to do so without a fight.

The minute the blindfold was gone, she felt blinded by the sudden light. Closing her eyes until they could adjust, she clawed at Hernando's face, even as he grabbed her arms and tried to pull them away. In that instant she heard the door smash open and a familiar voice cry out, "Let her go!"

Ramon? Her heart raced. Surely she was imagining things. There was no way Ramon could have found her. But as Hernando's grip lessened for a moment and she reopened her eyes, she was stunned to see that Ramon was indeed standing in the doorway.

Hernando quickly regained his composure. "Who are you?" he demanded, a sneer on his face. "And why should I let this woman go? She belongs to me."

Ramon shook his head. "She belongs to God," he said, stunning Julia with the confidence she heard in his voice. But even as a tiny spark of hope leapt in her heart, she saw someone come up behind Ramon, and she knew it was another one of her captors.

"Look out!" she screamed. "Behind you, Padre!"

Ramon spun around and ducked just as the man leveled a gun at his chest and fired. The bullet missed him by inches, sailing straight into Hernando's side instead. Before the man could fire again, Julia saw a heavy object swing through the air and hit him full force on the side of the head. The gunman dropped to the ground.

Hernando, on the floor holding his side and bellowing in pain, looked from Ramon to Julia and back again, disbelief mingling with agony on his face. Julia stepped around him and headed straight into Ramon's open arms.

"Oh, thank God," she cried. "Thank God! How in the world did you find me? I thought surely I would die in this awful place."

Through her tears, as Ramon stroked her hair and held her close, she saw Frank Barnes standing in the doorway, a stunned look on his face and a large piece of wood in his hand. She realized then what had happened to the shooter. A sense of relief washed over her, and she felt her knees buckle. She could hardly believe it. She was going to get out of here alive.

★ CHAPTER 31 ★

WE NEED TO GO," Frank said, even as Julia leaned on Ramon. "Someone will have heard that shot and reported it. And those other guys and their dog could come back any time."

Ramon loosened his grip on Julia and looked back at Frank. "You're right. Let's get her out of here. Even if the *policia* do bother to show up, they don't like foreigners much."

In moments Julia was propped up in the backseat of the old Jeep, a blanket wrapped around her as they hurried back to La Paz. "How . . . how did you find me?" she asked at last, unable to contain her curiosity any longer.

Ramon told her the story of Itzel and her abuela, and Julia smiled, leaning her head back against the seat. Dear Itzel! She had seen her after all. And she'd had the courage to tell her abuela. That the dear old woman had then come to the compound to share the girl's story with the others was nothing short of a miracle.

A miracle. How many miracles must have come together for this to happen? Not only had she peered out the window of her captor's Blazer at the exact moment they were passing by Itzel, but the girl had seen her and reported it, and her grandmother had taken it to the next step. Still, that didn't explain how Ramon and Frank had found the place where she was being held.

She opened her mouth to ask, but Frank beat her to it. "Apparently it was your kidnappers' greed that brought us the rest of the way. Seems they thought they weren't going to get enough money from your family, so they decided to offer you to the local curanderos as a human sacrifice in hopes of getting a little more. Plus it solved their problem of getting rid of your . . . your body." His voice dropped at the end, and Julia knew he felt bad about what he'd said, but the fact that she would have died before this ordeal ended came as no surprise to her.

Ramon picked up the conversation then. "Most of the curanderos in the area don't take part in such things, but it is rumored that there are still a couple here and there who do. When the kidnappers put the word out on the street about what they were looking for, it got back to some of the curanderas in Chamula, who passed the information on to Itzel's grandmother. They even told her the name of the street where you were being held, since the kidnappers had left that contact information for the curanderas."

Julia watched from the backseat as he shrugged his shoulders. "All we had to do was find a house on that street with an old white Blazer."

"Good thing those guys hadn't left before we got there so we could see them driving away," Frank noted.

Ramon nodded. "And a very good thing that they left with their dog. Four men and a pit bull would be a lot for the two of us to go up against, no?"

Frank chuckled. "That's for sure. But not too much for God. After all, we could never have taken out the two guys who were still there without God's help."

Julia watched and listened to the exchange between the two men, as she became more and more aware of God's obvious intervention in her rescue.

I know the plans I have for you . . .

The words of the almost forgotten promise came drifting back, and she closed her eyes, exhausted but near tears at the realization that God truly did love and care for her.

★ ★ ★

IN A MATTER OF DAYS Julia was feeling strong and safe once again, and she looked forward to resuming classes with the children.

"Are you sure you don't want to take more time off?" Carolyn asked her as she visited with her one morning. "We would certainly understand. Besides, it will be Christmas soon, and we usually suspend classes for a couple of weeks then. You could just wait and start after that."

Julia shook her head as she poured tea for the two of them and then sat down at her tiny table to join her guest. "No. I want to get back to work as soon as I can. I can't wait to see the children again—especially Itzel."

Carolyn smiled. "I can imagine. They've all missed you, though we didn't go into detail with them about what happened. Some may know, simply because word spreads in these little communities. But few of them are willing to talk to the authorities from San Cristobal, so even if they come to Chamula looking for answers, I doubt anyone will tell them anything."

Julia sipped her tea and set the cup down. "Are you sure we shouldn't talk to them ourselves? I mean, won't they want to know what happened?"

Carolyn's dark eyes grew sad. "I asked Frank about that, and he said if it would do any good, we should. But word is already out on the street that the police have ignored the shooting and will allow the gang to settle things in their own way." She paused and laid a hand on Julia's. "That may mean they'll kill one or more of your captors, whoever they feel is responsible for letting you get away. But we also know from your parents that the gang got the initial payment of twenty thousand dollars, so that might explain the rumor that they've all moved out of the San Cristobal house and on to another area." She patted Julia's hand. "It isn't the same as at home, you know. No one will be prosecuted for any of this."

Julia nodded. It had been hard to accept, but she had come to understand that it's simply the way things were here, where strangers were not welcome and people held tightly to the old ways. She was the one invading their space, and she was the one who had to adjust her thinking accordingly.

She sighed. "I know you're right. And I know I need to let it go. But . . ." She hesitated before she asked, "Do you think they'll come after me again? They . . . they know I'm from the compound."

Carolyn squeezed Julia's hand. "I wish I could assure you that would never happen, and chances are good that it won't. They'll simply move on to someone else. But, Julia, there are no guarantees here—or anywhere, for that matter. We live in a dangerous world, a broken world, but we serve a mighty God. You know that now, don't you?"

Julia nodded again. She knew it as she'd never known it before. And though a lingering fear teased her in the night, she was learning to get past it as she renewed her prayer life and began once again to read her Bible.

She sighed. "My family wants me to come home. They don't want me to stay and finish my teaching commitment."

Carolyn lifted her eyebrows. "And what do you want to do?"

Julia hesitated. "I'm torn," she admitted. "I miss my kids and my parents. I thought about them almost constantly after I was kidnapped. And I understand why they want me to come home. To be honest, they never wanted me to come here in the first place. They were worried about my safety, and now look what's happened. The fact that I escaped doesn't make them feel much better."

"Maybe you should at least go home for a visit," Carolyn suggested.

"I've considered that. I even thought about going home for Christmas, especially since school will be out then anyway." She shook her head. "I just haven't decided yet."

Carolyn patted her hand again. "Whatever you decide, we'll stand by you."

The thought of the familiar Christmas decorations and carols and gatherings danced through Julia's mind, and she nearly made the decision to take Carolyn up on her offer. But the image of Padre Ramon's face stopped her.

She frowned. "Do you have a Christmas Eve service? Here at the compound, I mean."

Carolyn looked surprised. "Sure. It's a candlelight service, and nearly all our regular parishioners come. Sometimes guests come as well, people who would never come the rest of the year."

"I see." Her dreams of Christmas at home seemed to fade as she pictured the tiny La Paz chapel bathed in candlelight, with Padre Ramon playing his guitar and leading the singing. She realized she would have to think and pray a bit more before making her decision.

★ ★ ★

TYLER AND BRITTNEY had returned to school, relieved to know their mother was safe but still insisting that their grandparents join them in a continued campaign to get her to cut her time short and come home, once and for all.

Marie wasn't sure. True, there was nothing she'd like better than to have Julia back in the States, working at the high school once again and living just a few minutes away. And yet, if she'd learned anything in the midst of this horrible ordeal when she wondered if her daughter would even make it through alive, it was that she could no longer give lip service to her commitment to serve God—or to her desire to see her family do the same.

She sprayed the old cherry wood dining table and rubbed it with a soft cloth, breathing in the lemony fragrance. When she finished dusting she planned to retrieve a few Christmas decorations from the garage and start decorating. She and John usually did that during Thanksgiving weekend, but even with Tyler and Brittney there to help, they hadn't gotten around to it this year.

It never even entered our minds, she thought, giving a final swipe to one spot before moving on to the next. *We were far too busy worrying about what would happen to Julia and praying for her safe return.*

She sighed. *You rescued her, Lord. No thinking person could deny it. You intervened in so many miraculous ways and rescued her. But she's still there, still living in that dangerous, primitive place. What if she doesn't come back right away? What if she stays and something else happens to her?*

The memory of the many hours she'd spent in prayer—alone, with her husband, and with the prayer group from church—caused her to stop polishing the table. She stood still, remembering the joy she'd felt when they'd received the phone call that Julia had been found—that she was safe. She had been so certain that the gratitude and awe she'd felt at that moment would never escape her, that never again would she doubt God's faithfulness or care.

"Forgive me, Lord," she whispered. "Forgive my selfishness, please. I know she's Yours, not mine, and her life is in Your hands—at it should be. Help me to remember that, please."

What if I hadn't rescued her? What if she hadn't been found alive?

Marie's eyes widened, and she grabbed the back of a chair for support. What if . . .? What if Julia had died or never been found at all? What if they'd had to live the rest of their lives not knowing what had happened to their daughter?

She knew what God was asking her. Would she still love and trust Him then? Even then?

Tears pricked her eyes, and she closed them, breathing deeply to clear her mind. How was she to answer such a question? There really was only one acceptable answer, but how honest would it be if she gave it?

"You know my heart, Lord," she whispered at last. "I want to say I would trust You, no matter what, but I . . . I'm just not sure."

A sense of peace enveloped her, rather than the sense of condemnation she had expected. God did indeed know her heart . . . and He loved her anyway. She let the tears come then, grateful that it was God's faithfulness and not her own that made the difference.

★ CHAPTER 32 ★

ITZEL WAS EXCITED. It was Monday morning, and she would be returning to school at last. It had been almost two weeks since they'd had their Thanksgiving meal together with their teacher and Padre Ramon, and so much had happened since then.

She walked to school now beside her abuela, thinking of the awful day when she had seen the woman with the red hair, blindfolded yet peering out the window of the big white truck, the one Itzel knew belonged to the mean man who said the bad words. What if the men from La Paz hadn't rescued her? What would have happened to her then?

She'd overheard her abuela and two of her friends talking at the marketplace soon after the rescue. She knew she shouldn't have been listening, but she also knew they were talking about her teacher, and she wanted to know what they were saying. One of the curanderas said that great spirits must have protected her. Itzel thought that must surely be true, though she knew the people at the compound said there was only one great Spirit.

They arrived to find the gate open, and soon Itzel was seated at her desk, listening to Señora Bennington telling them about the next holiday they would celebrate. Itzel had thought nothing could be better than Thanksgiving, but the teacher talked about Christmas as if it would be the greatest day ever.

Itzel knew about Christmas—at least, she thought she did. Many celebrated Christmas in her village, even holding a great procession that wound its way through town toward the Church of San Juan. But Itzel's grandmother had

A CHRISTMAS GIFT

told her that though various Catholic saints were worshipped at that church, no priest was in attendance and no mass had been said in that place for many decades. The shamans and curanderos were in charge, as they were throughout the village.

"Now that you are all back," the teacher said, grabbing Itzel's attention, "we are going to decorate for Christmas so we can enjoy it and think about it for many days."

Itzel thought that sounded like a very nice idea. She had enjoyed helping with the decorating for Thanksgiving, and she looked forward to finding out how they would decorate for this next holiday.

By the end of the school day, when Itzel sat on the bench waiting for her abuela to pick her up, she found herself hoping that Señora Bennington would join her as she often did. She wasn't disappointed.

"Hello, Itzel," the señora said as she sat down next to her, the late afternoon sun warming them both. "I haven't had a chance to thank you for helping me." The woman laid her hand on Itzel's. The girl thought of drawing away, but she didn't. Señora Bennington's hand felt warm and soft. She liked it.

"I know God allowed us to see one another that day. If you hadn't seen me or told your abuela, I might never have been rescued. What you did was very brave."

At last she lifted her head, and their eyes met. Itzel was surprised to realize the woman's eyes were green. Hesitantly, she returned her teacher's smile. Itzel didn't think what she'd done had been so brave, but she was pleased to know that Señora Bennington thought so. She wanted to ask her what she meant when she said God had allowed them to see one another that day, but she couldn't make her mouth say the words.

"You and your abuela helped me so much," the woman said. "Thank you, Itzel. Thank you very, very much."

Itzel swallowed. She knew she needed to say something. At last she managed to speak, though even as she said the words she wondered why she had chosen them. "Christmas. I like Christmas."

Señora Bennington's face lit up, and her smile widened. "I'm glad to hear that. I like Christmas too. We will start working on our decorations tomorrow. Do you and your abuela go to the church in town on Christmas Eve?"

Itzel felt her cheeks flush. She hoped her teacher wouldn't think badly of her. Slowly she shook her head. "No. Abuela says she doesn't like what they do in the church. We . . . never go."

Julia nodded. "I see."

A thought seemed to form into words and push its way out before Itzel could stop it. "Do you go to church, Señora Bennington?"

The woman paused slightly, and Itzel hoped she hadn't said the wrong thing. Then her teacher smiled and pointed at the little chapel across the courtyard. "I go to that little church there, where Padre Ramon is the pastor."

Itzel glanced at the small building and then looked back at her teacher. "Will you go there on Christmas Eve?"

The señora's eyes grew wide, and Itzel felt her hand tense on hers before she answered. "I . . . I don't know yet, Itzel. Why do you ask?"

"Because I think I would like to go there on that night."

She heard her teacher gasp, and this time she was certain she had said the wrong thing. Hanging her head, she blinked back tears, waiting for a scolding that was sure to come.

Instead she felt her teacher move her hand to Itzel's shoulder. "Itzel, that would be wonderful. We would love it if you would come. And your abuela too."

Slowly Itzel raised her head. Had she heard the señora correctly? The woman's smile and shining eyes assured her that she had. In that moment she felt a pain she hadn't even realized she had leave her heart, and she smiled in return.

★ ★ ★

As THE DAYS OF DECEMBER PASSED BY, Julia sat out in her tiny patio area, wrapped in a shawl and wondering how she would tell her parents and children that she wouldn't be coming home for Christmas after all. She knew it was the perfect time to break away for a visit and to reassure their hearts that she was fine—though she knew they would try to talk her out of coming back to complete the school year. But that wasn't the reason she'd decided to stay. Though she knew it was quite possible that Itzel's grandmother would refuse to come or to bring Itzel to the Christmas Eve service at the La Paz chapel, Julia knew she had to be here in case they showed up.

She'd already confided in Carolyn that she planned to stay, and she fully intended to try calling her family that night to let them know. Christmas was only a week away now, and she couldn't leave them hanging any longer.

"It is cool tonight, no?"

The unexpected masculine voice startled her, and she looked up to see Padre Ramon standing a few feet from her, just beyond her patio area. The day had been clear and crisp, but now the sun had set and the evening chill had moved in.

She nodded. "Yes, it is," she agreed, indicating the chair next to her. "Care to join me, Padre?"

His smile was warm in the dim light that shone through her kitchen window behind her. "I would like that," he said as he sat down beside her. "But I would like it even more if you would call me Ramon instead of Padre."

Julia felt her cheeks warm. The kind pastor had mentioned this request to her a couple of times since her rescue, but she still had trouble with the change. "I suppose

I should," she said. "After all, you saved my life. I should call you whatever name you prefer." She offered a light chuckle, though she knew it sounded forced.

"It wasn't me. I couldn't have saved your life on my own, even with Señor Barnes's help. We didn't know where to start looking for you or what we would do if we found you." He turned toward her, sitting just close enough that she could see the sincerity in his dark eyes. "Only God could have directed us, and only He could have protected you as He did." He shook his head. "It is an amazing thing. Each time I think of how it happened, it humbles me that God allowed me to be part of it."

Captivated by his eyes, Julia nodded and swallowed. She too was in awe each time she thought of all the factors that came together to accomplish her successful rescue. "I know what you mean," she said at last. "I know without a doubt that it was God who enabled me to get through that horrible experience and to get back home safe and sound."

Ramon smiled. "Ah, so now you think of La Paz as home. That is very nice to know."

The warmth in Julia's cheeks intensified. "Well, my temporary home," she mumbled. "I meant . . ."

She stopped, knowing anything she said at that point would infringe on their near perfect moment.

"I know what you meant," he said, breaking the silence. "I know you still have a home in the States, where your family is. But . . . I would like to think that La Paz has become your second home." He leaned forward slightly. "You are welcome and loved here, you know."

Julia swallowed. She did know that, but she couldn't figure out what to say.

She didn't have to. Ramon changed the subject. "My children will be home in a couple of days and will be staying until after Christmas. I am so glad you will be here to meet them and get to know them. Marina is so excited that her brother and sister are coming home."

Julia felt herself relax. It was so much easier when the focus of conversation was on something or someone other than herself. "That's wonderful, Padre . . . er, Ramon." She smiled, as did he. "I've been looking forward to meeting them, and I know Marina can't wait to see them again."

Ramon's eyes took on a faraway look for a moment, but he brought himself back quickly. "Marina has suffered the most from the loss of her mother." He smiled then. "She has been sad for a very long time now. But lately I see her looking more cheerful." He nodded. "It is because of you. She likes you very much."

Julia felt her eyes widen. Was she reading more into his words than was there? Surely she was. Surely he was making a simple statement, not implying or suggesting anything. But what bothered her most was that his words had so quickly stirred up thoughts in her own mind that had no business being there.

She shivered and drew her shawl around her. "It's getting cold," she said, standing to her feet. "I think I'll go inside now. Thank you so much for stopping by, Padre."

"Ramon," he said, smiling as he stood to face her.

"Ramon," she echoed. "Good night."

★ ★ ★

BRITTNEY WAS SITTING AT HER DESK in the room she shared with her roommate, Chloe, though she hadn't seen the girl since the previous day. Brittney couldn't imagine how she managed to stay in school.

She sighed. It wasn't her problem. She'd tried talking to Chloe about it a couple of times and had been told to mind her own business. OK, fine. No more worrying about Chloe, though she would continue to pray for her, something she'd been doing a lot of lately. But right now she had studying to do, enough to keep her up for hours. If only she could concentrate! Christmas was just days away, and she couldn't wait to get home and spend it with her family—though she still wasn't sure if her mom would be there or not.

She glanced at the time on her cell phone. Not quite 9:00. Surely her grandparents were still awake.

She speed-dialed their number, and after three rings her grandmother answered.

"Grandma, did I wake you?"

Brittney could hear the smile in her grandmother's voice. "No, sweetheart, you didn't. Grandpa and I are just sitting here in front of the fire, talking. How are you? How's school?"

"Everything's fine," she assured her. "I was just thinking about Christmas."

"That's what your grandpa and I were talking about too. It's nearly here, isn't it? When will you and Tyler be here?"

"Probably on the twenty-second or twenty-third. Is that OK?"

"Of course it is. You know you two are welcome anytime. And your grandpa and I finished putting up all the Christmas decorations today—inside and out."

"The tree too?"

Her grandma laughed. "No, not the tree. We know how much you and Tyler like to pick it out and decorate it."

Brittney smiled. "Thanks, Grandma. You're right. It just wouldn't be Christmas if we couldn't help with the tree." She paused. "So . . . have you heard from Mom? Is she coming?"

The pause alerted Brittney that she probably wasn't going to like the answer. "Actually, she called just an hour or so ago. That's one of the things your grandpa and I were talking about."

"And?"

She heard her grandmother sigh. "And she's not coming. She says she needs to be there for the Christmas Eve service at the compound."

"Oh." Brittney rolled the news around in her mind for a moment before answering, surprising herself with her reaction. "I guess that's OK. It must mean she's getting over what happened, that she isn't too scared to stay there and finish the rest of her year."

Another pause. "I'm pleased to hear you say that, honey. We were just saying the same thing. And . . . well, we believe it's what God wants for her right now."

Brittney nodded, though she knew her grandmother couldn't see her. "You're probably right. But I want you to know that I haven't forgotten all the praying we did for Mom when she was missing, and . . ." She took a deep breath. "And I know God answered us. I also know I want to go to church with you and Grandpa on Christmas Eve. And even though I can't speak for Tyler, I think he might too."

She could tell her grandma was smiling again. "Thank you, sweetheart. That's great news. It's going to be a wonderful Christmas!"

★ EPILOGUE ★

CHRISTMAS CAROLS PLAYED SOFTLY in the background, piped from Padre Ramon's old boom box. Julia was the first to arrive in the dimly lit chapel that Christmas Eve, and she settled into a seat in the third row. She knew Padre Ramon would appear with his guitar soon, ready to welcome arriving worshippers with singing. But now she imagined he was in the tiny room off the sanctuary, praying.

Splashes of color from various local plants and flowers decorated the room. Many were variations of the ti plants that had caught Julia's attention the day she so foolishly wandered off alone into the forest. She closed her eyes. So much had happened in such a short time. Just a few months ago she'd felt at loose ends, without direction or purpose. Now, though she missed her family, she felt as if she'd truly come home, despite the terrifying ordeal she'd endured. She knew she was where she was supposed to be, doing what she was supposed to be doing, and it was a wonderful feeling.

Home. The word carried such varied meanings, so many implications—and raised such a vast array of emotions. She smiled at the memory of her conversation with her parents and children earlier that day. Not only were Tyler and Brittney there with their grandparents for Christmas, but they were all going to Christmas Eve service together—even Tyler.

"Señora?"

The familiar voice brought her back from her thoughts, and she opened her eyes and looked up. "Padre Ramon. Merry Christmas."

"Ramon," he reminded her. "And merry Christmas to you, too, señora."

She smiled. "Julia."

He lifted his eyebrows and then smiled and nodded. "Julia. Sí. Thank you."

After a brief pause, he broke away and moved to the front, turning off the boom box before picking up his guitar and settling onto his stool. He spent a moment tuning up, and then began to strum "Silent Night," even as a handful of parishioners entered the building.

Julia spotted Ramon's three children, making their way toward the front. As they passed her, Marina turned and waved, her smile lighting up her face. Julia knew how excited the girl was to have her older brother and sister home for a visit.

Lovely young people, she thought as she watched them all settle into the front row. She'd had a chance to spend a little time getting to know Cristina and Antonio since they arrived a few days earlier, and their time together had been delightful. How she looked forward to Tyler and Brittney getting to know Ramon's children one day soon!

The thought brought heat to her cheeks. Was she running ahead of God's plans for her life? Quite possibly, though she knew Marina would like nothing better than for her father and teacher to get together. She'd dropped more than one hint lately, usually in front of Antonio and Cristina. Julia had been embarrassed but noticed that Ramon's older children seemed to welcome their little sister's comments.

Her eyes fell on Ramon again, even as he lifted his head and met her gaze. The warmth she felt in the exchange was more than embarrassment or shyness; it was a welcome connection that she sensed could very well develop into much more.

"Merry Christmas, Julia."

Once again a greeting interrupted her thoughts, and she turned to see Frank and Carolyn slip into the two seats to her left.

"Merry Christmas to you," she replied. "This is absolutely beautiful! I'm so looking forward to the service tonight."

Carolyn nodded and patted her hand. "We are too. And we're so pleased that you decided to stay here for Christmas. I'm sure it wasn't an easy decision, knowing you could be home with your family."

Julia smiled. "You're right. It wasn't easy. But I knew this was where God wanted me to be, and that's all that matters. Besides, I really do feel like I'm home, right here, with my family and friends."

Carolyn's eyes glistened and she reached out and pulled Julia into a hug. "We feel exactly the same way about you, Julia."

The room was filling up then, with only a few seats left. Julia had purposely sat in the middle of the row, with two seats on each side of her. Now that Frank and Carolyn had taken the ones to her left, she wondered if she should set her shawl and Bible on the two on her right. She so hoped Itzel and her grandmother would show up, and she wanted to have seats for them if they did.

She glanced back anxiously, knowing it was nearly time for the service to begin. The room was almost completely full, and her heart sank as she noticed that the two she watched for were not among the stragglers.

And then she saw them—peering shyly inside, eyes scanning the room. Without thinking, Julia stood to her feet and waved. Itzel's face lit up, and she and her grandmother quickly made their way up the aisle to sit beside Julia.

Abuela nodded in greeting but said nothing, while Itzel shyly received the hug Julia offered.

"I'm so glad you came," Julia whispered. "Merry Christmas."

Itzel nodded. "It will be a good Christmas. The best." She dropped her eyes and then lifted them again. Tears mirrored her emotions. "It is the best because you are here with us. I don't ever want you to leave."

A sharp pain stabbed Julia's heart. The girl wanted her to stay forever—to never leave. That was not a promise she could make. But was it a possibility?

She took Itzel's hand in hers and squeezed it. Just a few weeks earlier she'd been tied to a chair, wondering if she would live or die and wishing for nothing more than to go home to her parents and children. Now, though she knew she wanted to see her family again, she also found her heart leaning toward a new life, right here at La Paz—and not just for a few more months, but indefinitely.

"*Feliz Navidad,*" Padre Ramon called out, and then he began the first song as the congregation stood. Once again his eyes found hers, and she felt her heart swell.

"Feliz Navidad," she mouthed back to him. *Merry Christmas, Ramon.*

There was no way for her to know what lay ahead, but she knew the God who did. And that was the greatest Christmas gift anyone could ever receive.

New Hope® Publishers is a division of WMU®, an international organization that challenges Christian believers to understand and be radically involved in God's mission. For more information about WMU, go to wmu.com. More information about New Hope books may be found at NewHopeDigital.com New Hope books may be purchased at your local bookstore.

Please go to
NewHopeDigital.com
for the book club guide for *A Christmas Gift.*

If you've been blessed by this book,
we would like to hear your story.
The publisher and author welcome your comments and
suggestions at: newhopereader@wmu.org.